THIS BOOK
BELONGS TO

Michelle

ABOUT THE AUTHOR

Duncan Ball began work as an industrial chemist but he'd always wanted to be a writer or a painter. In his spare time he wrote an adult novel and soon he'd given away work in science to began writing the popular books for children that he now writes full time.

Duncan's second novel, *Selby's Secret*, exploring the wonderful world of Selby (the only talking dog in Australia and, perhaps, the world), proved such a success that its fans demanded more and more Selby adventures — which Duncan has been happy to supply. The Selby saga now comprises six collections of nearly one hundred short stories (all beautifully illustrated by Allan Stomann), and the musical play, *Selby the Talking Dog*. The Selby books have been published overseas in New Zealand, Japan, Germany and the USA and have won and been short-listed for many awards — most of them voted by the children themselves.

Duncan has also written other books for children including three books about Emily Eyefinger (who was born with an eye on the end of her finger), three books about the diabolical tricks of the cunning and cranky ghost of Arnold Taylor (including *The Ghost and the Goggle Box*), six easy-to-read 'Skinny Mysteries' (including *The Case of the Graveyard Ghost*), and some picture books (including the ever-popular *Jeremy's Tail*, illustrated by Donna Rawlins).

When Duncan isn't writing books he is working on television scripts, painting, bushwalking or answering the many letters he receives. (To reach him write care of HarperCollins at the address in the front of this book.)

For more information about Duncan and his books boot up your computer and surf your way to Selby's website at: **http://www.selby.aust.com** — see you there!

BY THE SAME AUTHOR

SELBY
SNOWBOUND

DUNCAN BALL

illustrated by Allan Stomann

HarperCollinsPublishers

For Jillaroo
My bulwark, my ramparts and often my keep.

The author would like to thank all of those wonderful Selby fans who have written to him over the years. And a very special thanks to one of them, Brendan Watts, who suggested that Dr Trifle invent a machine to teach the non-swimming Selby how to swim. Dr Trifle doesn't usually take advice from anyone but when he heard this he thought 'Why not?'. For the results see the story called 'The Paddle-Pup'.

HarperCollins*Publishers*

First published in Australia in 1998
Reprinted in 1998, 1999
by HarperCollins*Publishers* Pty Limited
ACN 009 913 517
A member of the HarperCollins*Publishers* (Australia) Pty Limited Group
http://www.harpercollins.com.au

Some of these stories were published in shorter form in the Australian edition of
Family Circle magazine.

HarperCollins*Publishers*
25 Ryde Road, Pymble, Sydney, NSW 2073, Australia
31 View Road, Glenfield, Auckland 10, New Zealand
77–85 Fulham Palace Road, London W6 8JB, United Kingdom
Hazelton Lanes, 55 Avenue Road, Suite 2900, Toronto, Ontario M5R 3L2
and 1995 Markham Road, Scarborough, Ontario M1B 5M8, Canada
10 East 53rd Street, New York NY 10032, USA

National Library of Australia Cataloguing-in-Publication data:

Ball, Duncan, 1941–   .
Selby snowbound.
ISBN 0 207 19652 4.
1. Dogs – Juvenile fiction. 2. Adventure stories. I. Allan Stomann. II. Title.
A823.3

Printed in Australia by Griffin Press Pty Ltd on 80gsm Econoprint

10 9 8 7 6 5 4 3   99 00 01 02 03

AUTHOR'S NOTE

These are Selby's stories, not mine. They're all things that happened to him. He later rang me up and told them to me and I retold them as best I could.

As you probably know, Selby's real name isn't Selby and his owners aren't really called Dr and Mrs Trifle and the town he lives in isn't called Bogusville. He made all those things up so no one can find him. Because he's the only talking dog in Australia and, perhaps, the world, he knows that if people knew where he lived it would ruin his life forever. He won't even tell *me* his real name or where he lives.

You may think that he's really a person and he only tells me on the telephone that he's a dog. But it's not true — I actually met him and we even had dinner together in a restaurant. Of course he didn't want to give away his secret so he wore a disguise: a dog suit. The other people in the restaurant thought that he was a *person* wearing a dog suit (which isn't that unusual) but, of course, he was really a talking dog in a dog suit.

How could I be sure it was him? Once, during the meal, he reached for the salt and suddenly the glove part of the dog suit separated slightly from the sleeve part — and guess what? Fur! A furry dog leg inside the dog suit. Oh yes, it was him all right.

As he munched his way through three platters of peanut prawns, he told me more stories about himself. Some of them are in this book. I hope you like them.

DUNCAN BALL

CONTENTS

Slow Pup

Climbing a mountain always begins with a **slope up**. And I'm a **slow pup** so I guess I must be a good mountain-climber. Does that make sense? Anyway, read the story about being snowbound and you'll see how I, Selby, myself, me, personally climbed the highest mountain in the world!

But there are lots of other exciting stories in this book and I don't want to spoil it by telling you too much.

So turn off the TV, sit back and get ready for a mountain of fun!

Cya,

🐾 Selby

NURSE SELBY

'I'm sorry, Selby, but you'll have to stay right here,' Mrs Trifle said. 'They don't allow dogs in hospitals. But don't worry, I won't be long.'

Selby watched as Mrs Trifle went inside to inspect the new wing of Bogusville Hospital.

'It's not fair,' he thought. 'Why can't I go in too? I watch all those hospital shows on TV but I've never been inside a real live hospital. I'm sooooo curious. Curiosity is about to kill this dog.'

Selby curled up under a park bench. Next to him was an old copy of the *Bogusville Banner* that he'd found. He began secretly reading it for something to do.

'This is silly. I'm going to go in there anyway. Seeing me will be good for the patients. Pets cheer people up and sick people need cheering up. Anyway, what can happen if I get caught?

1

They'll only kick me out, that's all. I'm out right now so if they catch me I'll be right back where I am.'

'Hmmm,' Selby hmmmed. 'I wonder how I can sneak in?'

Suddenly an ambulance with its siren screaming tore up to the door marked CASUALTY and screeched to a stop.

'This is my chance,' Selby thought as the ambulance attendants wheeled the patient through the door. 'While they're busy I'll just nip through the door and no one will notice.'

Selby crept around the bushes beside the hospital wall and then trotted in through the open door.

'So far, so good,' he thought as he rounded the corner into a ward. 'Now for a look at a real hospital. It certainly does look like the ones on TV.'

Selby trotted around looking at all the people in the beds. A man in a wheelchair stopped in the corridor and gave him a pat and a little girl climbed out of bed to give him a cuddle.

'Oh, that's nice,' he thought. 'And it's good for me too. It makes me feel wanted. Everyone likes to feel wanted — and so does every*dog*.'

Selby went along from room to room looking at everything. Until suddenly he saw Mrs Trifle coming towards him. She was walking down through a ward with a group of doctors and nurses.

'Ooops!' he thought, ducking into a storeroom. 'I'll just hide in here till they go by.'

Selby waited for a minute until he noticed another door at the back of the storeroom with a round window in it.

'Maybe I can nip out that way,' he thought. 'I wonder where it goes.'

Selby put his paws up on the door and peered through the glass.

'It's an operating theatre!' Selby thought. 'This is great! And look! 🐾 they're actually operating on someone in there. Oh wow, now I can see a real operation!'

Selby watched as a surgeon gave last minute instructions to her operating team.

🐾 *Paw note: This exclamation mark has a comma at the bottom so you can use it in the middle of a sentence. It's my new invention.*

'Maybe if I just open the door a little I can hear what she's saying,' Selby thought, pushing the door open a crack.

'As you know, the patient has lost all function in his left orbital *glandula solletico* — or tickle gland, as we know it,' the surgeon said. 'Tickle him under the left arm and nothing happens. Today we are going to attempt the impossible — we're going to make him ticklish again. If this operation works, Bogusville Hospital could become the worldwide centre for tickle research. The patient is now unconscious so let's get started.'

'Oh, boy!' Selby thought as the surgeon started cutting into the patient. 'I wish I could get closer. I can't see properly.'

Suddenly Selby spied a stack of operating theatre gowns hanging on hooks beside him.

'I'll just slip into one of these,' he said, putting one on. 'And now one of those little round caps that I can pull down over my ears, and an operating theatre mask, and then some gloves to cover my paws.'

In a second Selby had his cap pulled down so low and his mask pulled up so high that the only part of his face you could see was his eyes.

Quietly he pushed the door open and walked on his hind legs into the operating theatre.

'This is so much fun! They're so busy they won't notice me,' Selby thought as, one by one, each of the surgeon's helpers held clamps inside the patient and pulled tubes this way and that. 'If I squint a bit the blood and gore won't bother me.'

Suddenly the surgeon turned to Selby. 'You're just in time, nurse,' she said. 'We're a little short-handed today. Could you pass me the Dweeb-Meyer Impaling Key, please?'

'I beg your pardon?' Selby said out loud without thinking.

'Just hand me the Dweeb-Meyer.'

Selby looked at the instruments all laid out in a row on a tray.

'Quickly, nurse,' the surgeon said. 'The patient's pulse is dropping. We don't want to lose him.'

Selby reached down and picked up something that looked like a large corkscrew and handed it to the surgeon.

'No, no, not the Thurthmail Extractor! I said the Dweeb . . . Hang on a tick. You're right! If I use the Thurthmail I can go up through the *osso isterico* — the funny bone. Good thinking, nurse.'

'Oh, no!' Selby thought as the surgeon went to work twisting the corkscrew-like instrument into the patient's elbow. 'I've got to get out of here before I faint!'

'Capitulatory Ventriculator!' the surgeon said, holding out her hand.

'Sorry?' Selby said.

'Nurse, could you please hand me the Capitulatory Ventriculator and make it snappy!'

Selby picked up an instrument that looked like a baby's rattle and handed it to the surgeon.

'Nurse, don't you know the difference between a Capitulatory Ventriculator and a Bradwell Bone Splinterer?' the surgeon demanded.

'Well yes, but —' Selby started.

'Ahah!' the surgeon said as her eyes lit up. 'So you're saying that I should *splinter* instead of *ventriculating*. Maybe you're right. Okay, here goes.'

Selby edged towards the door.

'Oh, no!' Selby thought. 'Now she's going to splinter when she should be ventriculating — and all because of me! She thinks I'm a real operating theatre nurse! She thinks I know what I'm talking about! Get me out of here!'

'The Freebuschram, please,' the surgeon said.

'Come on now, nurse, the patient is waking up.'

Selby grabbed something that looked like a gardening trowel on one end and a toilet plunger on the other. The surgeon stood there in shock for a second and then her eyes brightened.

'Good thinking!' she cried, snatching the instrument from Selby's paw. 'The Fingaloose

7

is a much better choice than a Freebuschram. What's your name, sister?'

'I — I — I,' Selby stammered.

'Come on, don't be shy.'

'Sel —' Selby started. 'Selina.'

'Well, Selina, you certainly have a lot of surgical experience,' the surgeon said as she finished with the Fingaloose and stitched up the patient. 'By the way, have you ever thought of fixing that honker?'

'That what?'

'That nose of yours. I could give you a real movie star's nose if you wanted. And I could also get rid of that facial hair around your eyes. You are a bit furry, if you don't mind my saying so.'

'No, thanks anyway,' Selby said, backing towards the door, 'but my fur is my best feature.'

'Well, suit yourself. But if you ever change your mind —'

'Doctor!' one of the nurses exclaimed. 'The patient is coming to.'

'Oh, good,' said the surgeon. 'Let's give him the tickle test and see how we've done. Go ahead, give him a little tiddly diddly under the arm.'

Selby slipped out of the operating theatre and listened to the patient's screams of laughter. In a minute Selby was out of his gown, out of the hospital, and lying innocently under the bench once again.

'Boy, I'm glad that's over,' he thought as he waited for Mrs Trifle. 'It was great to see a real operation but it was also a very close call for me. I won't be doing that again soon. I guess you'd say that the whole thing was *a very ticklish operation*!'

SELBY LOVESTRUCK

Selby was madly in love.

It all began when the Trifles left Selby at home when they went on holidays. Of course they didn't know that he was the only talking dog in Australia and, perhaps, the world, and that he could look after himself when they were away. So they asked Aunt Jetty to drop around to fill Selby's bowl with Dry-Mouth Dog Biscuits from time to time.

Selby spent his days reading, playing with the computer and watching lots and lots of TV. All of which would have been perfectly wonderful if Selby hadn't fallen madly in love with a beautiful actress called Bonnie Blake.

Bonnie was the incredibly talented and beautiful mega TV soapie star of a series called *Restless Hearts Aflame*. But the day Selby fell in love he was watching her being interviewed on another show called *Your Lucky Stars*.

'She's such a wonderful actress,' Selby sighed. 'And she's *soooooooooooo* beautiful! Just looking at her makes my little heart go pitter-patter-pitter-pat. And when she speaks she's so sweet that I just want to faint.'

'Tell me, Miss Blake —' the interviewer began.

'Please call me Bonnie,' the actress interrupted. 'I'm no one special. I'm really just a normal average girl-next-door.'

'Oh, how I wish she was the girl next door to me!' Selby squealed.

'Well then, Bonnie. May I ask you some personal questions?'

'Nothing is too personal. I'm an actress and I belong to the world,' Bonnie said. 'I suppose you want to talk about my break-up with Todd Delvane?'

'Yes. What went wrong between you and Todd?'

'Oh, I don't know,' Bonnie sighed. 'He was an actor, too, you know. I think he became jealous of my fame. That's when — I don't know how to say this because Todd is such a dear sweet person — but that's when his life went out of control.'

'Was he cruel to you?'

11

'Yes. I finally had to ask him to leave.'

'If I ever see that Todd guy,' Selby thought, 'I'll bite him into next week! How could he be cruel to such a wonderful sensitive person?'

'He was your sixth husband, is that right?' the interviewer asked.

'I don't know — I guess so.'

'And you have had six husbands in only five years.'

'They were all very nice men,' Bonnie said. 'But none of them could handle my fame. It's been a difficult time. Then I lost Tiddles.'

'Tiddles? Was he a — friend?'

'He was my dog.'

'And you never found him?'

'No, I don't mean that sort of lost. Tiddles fell off the balcony of my apartment.'

'Was it a long way down?'

'Yes. I live on the thirty-fourth floor.'

'So he's —'

'Dead,' Bonnie sniffed.

Tears formed in Bonnie's eyes and in Selby's at the same time.

'I didn't buy him,' she added. 'He just came into my life. It was fate. I was taking my evening walk by the beach and there he was, lost and hungry. I took him home and tried to find his owners but I couldn't. He must have lost his collar. That little dog became the most loving friend I've ever had.'

'Oh, how I'd love to be Bonnie's loving dog-friend,' Selby thought. The tears now streamed down his face. 'I mean I love the Trifles but they're like parents to me. What I need is someone like Bonnie. Oh, how I wish I could marry her and live happily ever after.'

'Tiddles meant so much to me that — I know this will sound stupid — but I wish I could have married him.'

'I don't think they let people marry dogs,' the interviewer said.

'I know, but if I could find a dog that could talk, he would be my dream companion. There would be no silly career jealousies or competing with each other.'

'If you had a talking dog I'm afraid he'd get much more attention than you,' the interviewer laughed. 'He'd be on the news all over the world every day. You'd have reporters camped on your doorstep. You'd never get any peace.'

'You're right,' Bonnie sighed. 'What I really want is a dog who can talk but who keeps it a secret from everyone but me.'

'If I ever hear of one, I'll tell you,' the interviewer laughed.

'Yes, I know it's an impossible dream but that's where my heart is right now.'

'You mean a *possible* dream!' Selby shouted at the TV. 'And I am your dream dog! Oh, lucky me! I've just found my dream companion! Now all I have to do is ring her up and tell her that I'm a talking dog and that I'm in love with her. Hmmm, let's see now, she lives in one of those high-rise apartments at Bandicoot Bay. I'll see if she's in the phone book. But, hold the show! She won't believe that I'm a dog. The only way to do this is to go there so that she can see that I'm a real live talking feeling dog.'

And so it was that Selby crept into the luggage compartment of a Bandicoot Bay-bound bus and bounced around all night till the bus reached the Bay.

'Now to find Bonnie's apartment,' Selby thought as he looked at the photos he'd torn from a fan magazine. 'Ahah! There it is: the apartment block with the pink flamingo painted on the side. This is going to be easy.'

Selby raced along the footpath to the front

door but, as he entered, a man in a doorman's suit came rushing toward him.

'Where do you think you're going?!' the man yelled.

Selby turned and ran out again, feeling the doorman's boot hit his bottom as he did.

Soon the sun set and a cold rain began to fall. Selby was now too weak and exhausted to even think of catching the bus back.

'Why did I come here?' he thought. 'I should have known that a mega TV soapie star would have a doorman to keep undesirables — and dogs — away. This is the stupidest thing I've ever done. I'll just have a snooze and then catch the bus to Bogusville in the morning.'

Selby lay down. He felt the hard ground under him. He trembled all over and hunger pangs gripped his stomach. He drifted in and out of a dream.

Suddenly a hand reached out and touched him.

'Oh, you poor dear. Are you all right?' a sweet voice asked. 'How did you get here? What's wrong? Are you okay? You look hungry and tired and cold. Let me take you home with me.'

Selby turned his tired head to one side. It was

her! Bonnie Blake! And she was putting her coat around him and lifting him into her arms.

The next thing Selby knew he was in Bonnie's apartment.

'Oh, you poor dear,' she said again, putting a plate of real people-food in front of him. 'Here, eat this. I'll run a good hot bath for you. Oh, what a wonderful little guy you are.'

'This is it!' Selby thought. 'This is my big chance! I *have* to talk to her!'

And so it was that Selby finally said the near-fatal words: 'Bonnie, I think I love you.'

'You — you — what?!' the startled star said. 'Did you just speak?'

'Yes, I did, Bonnie.'

'But dogs can't speak!'

'I am the only talking dog in Australia and, perhaps, the world.'

'B-But how did you learn to talk?'

'It just happened. I was watching TV and suddenly I could understand everything. Then I taught myself to talk.'

'Were you watching *Restless Hearts Aflame*?'

'No, it was before that,' Selby admitted.

'And where do you live?'

'In a little town called Bogusville. My owners

don't know that I know how to talk. You're the only one who does. Can I live with you from now on?'

'And be my loving friend?'

'You've got it.'

'Oh, Selby darling,' Bonnie gushed. 'Now I can stop my never-ending search for a gentle kind considerate man — because I know there aren't any anyway.'

'It'll be just me and you, Bonnie baby.'

'Yes, but you have to promise me one thing, Sel darling.'

'That I'll never tell anyone that I can talk, is that it?' Selby said.

'How did you guess?'

'I heard you say it on TV. Of course I won't, Bonnie darling.'

'Oh Selby, Selby, Selby,' Bonnie said, kissing Selby gently on the lips. 'You are the most wonderful being on this whole crazy planet.'

In the days that followed, every morning Bonnie went off to the studio while Selby lazed around watching video tapes of every episode of *Restless Hearts Aflame*.

In the evening, Bonnie would cook fabulous

meals and then they'd sit together holding hands and paws and gazing into each other's eyes.

But then one day when Bonnie was about to leave for work she said: 'Oh, Selly-belly baby?'

'Yes, Bon-bon?' Selby responded.

'Would little Selby-welby mind awfully-waffly making din-dins for us tonight?'

'Of course I wouldn't mind. I think I saw some recipe books on the shelf. I think I can follow a recipe.'

'Oh, and would you make the beddy-weddies?'

'Yes, darling Bonnie-wonnie.'

Bonnie stood there in the doorway, smiling and blinking her long curvy eyelashes.

'And could you do some sweeping and mopping and vacuuming and then wash the windows and polish the furniture?' she asked.

'Yes, of course, darling.'

'Oh and, Sel?'

'Yes, Bon?'

'Could you clean the toilet?'

'The toilet? For you, my dear, I would do anything.'

However, day after day Selby found that he was doing more and more work. Sometimes when Bonnie arrived home he didn't even feel like a cuddle because he was so exhausted. Bonnie had him writing cheques to pay the bills and phoning people to make appointments for her with her hairdresser and her manicurist.

And then one fateful day Bonnie said: 'Selby,' (she didn't call him 'Sel', or 'darling', or 'dear', or 'Selby-welby', just 'Selby') 'how are you going to earn some money? I mean, so far, I've earned all the money around here. Isn't it about time you helped out? Think about it.'

'I just thought about it, Bonnie,' Selby said, sort of snappily (without saying 'Bon-bons', or 'Bonsie-wonsie', or 'Bonnie-poo'), 'and I don't like the idea. Besides, how could I possibly get a job?'

'You could tell everyone you can talk and then get acting parts for talking dogs on TV. I could be your agent. We'd make a bomb. Then I could retire and just lie around the way you do.'

'Lie around?! Are you kidding?! I run myself ragged all day long just to give you a comfortable home! I cleaned the toilet three times this week you didn't even notice! You don't appreciate me.'

Bonnie gave him an icy stare.

'What kind of dog are you?' she asked.

'I'm a good dog, basically. I mean, I try to be a good dog but you've pushed me too far!'

'I don't mean that. I mean what *kind* of dog are you, a beagle or something?'

'No, I'm not a beagle. I'm bigger than a beagle.'

'But you're still a *short* dog. You're not one of those tall handsome dogs like an Alsatian or a Russian wolfhound.'

'Okay, so I'm short. You knew I was short when you met me. You didn't mind it then.'

'It's just *you* I mind. You remind me of my sixth husband.'

'Well, I feel sorry for him. I feel sorry for all of them! I'll bet you drove them all bonkers. Come to think of it, I wouldn't be surprised if Tiddles didn't *fall* off that balcony of yours. He probably jumped!'

Bonnie's lip curled, her eyes narrowed and her nostrils flared.

'You're right,' she said, suddenly lifting Selby up and carrying him onto the balcony. 'He didn't fall.'

'You threw him off!' Selby screamed. 'You killed him because he wouldn't wait on you hand and foot! Put me down, you murderer!'

'I'll put you down, all right — thirty-four storeys down. *Look out below*!' she screamed.

Selby could feel the wind whistling past his ears. Suddenly he felt the hard ground under him. He trembled all over and hunger pangs gripped his stomach. He drifted in and out of a dream.

Suddenly a hand reached out and touched him.

'Oh, you poor dear. Are you all right?' It was Bonnie's sweet voice. 'How did you get here? What's wrong? Are you okay? You look hungry and tired and cold.'

'It's her again!' Selby thought. 'First she tried to kill me and now she's going to be nice to me! She's a stark, raving loony!'

'Oh, you poor little doggy-woggy.'

'Now hang on,' Selby thought. 'I don't think I was dropped off that building after all. If I did, I'd be dead. I must have been dreaming all that stuff about me and Bonnie ever since I lay down here. Why I haven't been in her apartment at all!'

'Let me take you home with me,' Bonnie said as she started to pick him up.

'Oh, no you don't!' Selby said, and he broke free.

'You talked! Good grief! I just heard you talk!'

'Of course I talked! Now get away from me!'

'But you're what I've been looking for all my life! You'd be my dream companion! Oh, please please come back to me.'

'Not on your life!' Selby yelled over his shoulder as he started to run. 'You'd have me cleaning toilets in no time.'

'Toilets? What are you talking about?'

'You'll say you won't but I can't take that chance from now on. From now on I'm going to be my own dog and nobody's ever going to boss me around!'

And in a few minutes Selby was back on the Bogusville-bound bus, bumping around in the luggage compartment again. And the next morning he saw Bonnie on the TV news telling an interviewer about the talking dog she'd just seen.

(Of course nobody believed her.)

'She's *sooooo* beautiful!' Selby thought. 'And she's probably a wonderful person. But I guess I'll never know because I'm going to stay with the Trifles forever. They are my real dream companions.'

SELBY SUPER-SELLER

The Trifles were out of the house and Selby was watching his favourite TV learning program called *You Can Sell Anything!*

'I just love the way this Harold Huckster guy explains how to be a super-salesperson,' Selby thought. 'I'd love to give it a go. I'd love to go around knocking on doors, selling encyclopaedias, and things to clean carpets, and all that greasy stuff that women put on their faces. It would be so much fun.'

'And this brings us to the end of another program,' Harold announced. 'So what have we learned? What are today's Steps to Success? First, confuse your customers. When they're confused you can have them eating out of the palm of your hand.'

'Got it, Harold,' Selby thought. 'What next?'

'And don't forget to flatter them. Make them feel good about themselves and they'll do anything you want.'

'And then?' Selby thought.

'And then,' Harold said, 'remember that before you sell a product you have to sell *yourself*. And to sell yourself all you have to do is smile. Get that smile right and they'll believe anything you say. So, until next time — happy smiling and happy selling!'

'Here's how I'd do it,' Selby said, practising a huge smile in front of the mirror. Then he put on a cheerful voice. 'Hello, my name's Selby. What a lovely house you have. I know you're busy and that's why I'm here. I have just the thing to make your life easy. And for today only we have a special never-to-be-repeated offer. Hi, my name's Selby. G'day, I'm Selby.'

Selby heaved a great sigh.

'I could never be a salesperson,' he said, 'because I can never be a person. But it's still fun to pretend. Hi, I'm Selby. G'day.'

Selby smiled a big smile and then an even bigger one. But it still didn't look right.

'It's no good,' he thought as he headed off on his afternoon walk. 'Better to start with a little smile that gets bigger and bigger till it breaks like an ocean wave into a huge smile. I could start with just a twinkle in my eye. Everybody likes an eye twinkle. Then I'd slide slowly into a glamorous grin with just a touch of frown. No teeth showing yet. Then I'd hit them with a super-spectacular ear-to-ear all-over-my-face smile. Hi, I'm Selby and this is your lucky day. Have I got the perfect product for all your household needs. It just costs a few cents a day. Please allow me to explain —'

Selby was smiling his way across the street just trying out his super-spectacular ear-to-ear all-over-his-face smile when suddenly he heard the sound of screeching brakes. The next thing he knew he was flying through the air and then lying beside the road. Selby's head was spinning as a man and woman jumped out of the car.

'The poor thing,' the woman said. 'Did you see that ? ❦ he wasn't watching where he was going.'

❦ *Paw note: This is my newly-invented question-comma. You can use it in the middle of sentences. Good, hey?* S

26

'That's the problem with these small towns,' the man said. 'No one's used to traffic because there never is any. Even their pets cross the streets without looking.'

'Oooooooh,' Selby moaned out loud. 'What happened?'

The man and woman stood open-mouthed staring down at him.

'I beg your pardon,' the woman said.

'Where am I?' Selby asked.

'You're in some awful little town,' the man said. 'We're just passing through. I think I saw a sign that said Doughnutville or something like that. By the way,' he added, 'do you realise that you just talked?'

'Did I?'

'You not only did but you're still doing it.'

'So what?'

'So, you're a dog and dogs don't talk.'

'Well you're obviously wrong because *I* do,' Selby said, still dazed and confused and wondering where he was.

Slowly the man and woman turned to each other and smiled a couple of smiles that were even more super-spectacular and ear-to-ear and all-over-their-faces than Selby's best smile.

'Are you thinking what I'm thinking?' the man asked the woman.

'If you're thinking that this is the greatest thing that's ever happened to us in our whole lives, then I guess I am thinking what you're thinking,' she answered.

'He's a real live talking dog!' the man exclaimed. 'We are going to be rich! We could be staring down the barrel of a billion bucks! We now own the world's *only* talking dog! I'll never have to do any of those stupid TV shows again!'

'Own?' Selby thought as the world kept spinning around him. 'Did they say that they *own* me?'

'Quick! Chuck him in the boot and let's get out of here!' the man said.

'But someone might miss him.'

'Who cares? Anyone who lets a talking dog walk freely around the streets without bodyguards has got bubble gum for brains. Someone could just come along and dognap him, couldn't they? Heh-heh-heh. Get what I mean? Huh? Huh?'

'Gotcha,' the woman said, giving an evil little grin and an even more evil giggle.

'Dognap?' Selby thought. 'Are they kidding? Hey, he's grabbing my leg! Now he's grabbing another leg! Now she's grabbing the rest of my legs. I think I'm being dognapped!'

As they lifted him into the boot, the man suddenly smiled again and something clicked in Selby's brain.

'I know who the dude is!' he thought. 'He's Harold Huckster! I'd recognise that smile anywhere! I'm being dognapped by a television personality! Oh, woe, why did I talk? But it's too late now — I've already done it. Now my only chance is to bite and kick and scratch and run away. But I can't — I'm so dizzy that I can't even walk!'

'We're going to be billionaires,' Harold snickered as he began to close the boot. He paused. 'Maybe even *grillionaires*! We'll sell his story to TV! We'll put him in commercials! We'll sell tickets for people to come to talk to him! Then we'll teach him to sing and he'll be the most famous pop star in history!'

'Oh, woe, if only I could talk them out of thinking that I can talk,' Selby thought. 'But how could I do that when I've already talked?'

'You forgot about making him a movie star and keeping all the money,' the woman said, brushing her hair back with her fingers.

'I know,' Selby thought. 'This is a job for Selby Super-Seller. Only this time I'm not selling a product — I'm selling an idea. I have to *sell* them the *idea* that I didn't really talk.

Hmmm, how will I do it? I've got it! I'll just follow Harold Huckster's Steps to Success. First, confuse them, then flatter them and then sell yourself. Only how can I *sell* myself when I've already *given* myself away? Oh well, here goes.'

Suddenly Selby flashed a little eye twinkle at Mr and Mrs Huckster.

'Hi, there,' he said, putting out his paw. 'I'm Selby and I'm pleased to meet you.'

'And I'm Harold Huckster,' Harold said, automatically putting out his hand to shake Selby's paw and then quickly pulling it back. 'Hey, what's going on here?'

'Have you ever seen a talking dog before, Harold?' Selby asked.

'Well no, I haven't,' Harold said, looking slightly puzzled.

'I think I've got him confused,' Selby thought. 'Now to start selling myself.'

'Why do you think that is, Harold?' Selby said, breaking into a glamorous grin with a touch of frown.

'W-Well I don't know,' the salesman said, getting more baffled by the second.

'Could it be,' Selby said, suddenly bursting

31

into his super-spectacular ear-to-ear all-over-his-face smile, 'that it's because *they don't exist*?'

'D-Don't they?' the man stammered, watching helplessly as the suddenly-not-so-dizzy Selby climbed out of the boot.

'This is it!' Selby thought. 'Now it's time to flatter them.'

'You people look like highly intelligent people to me,' Selby said aloud.

'Yes, I guess we are,' Harold Huckster said.

'And any intelligent person knows that dogs can't talk, isn't that right?'

'W-W-Well that's right,' Mrs Huckster said.

'This is great!' Selby thought. 'I've got them eating out of the palm of my hand — or out of the palm of my paw, anyway.'

'Now just a minute,' Mrs Huckster said. 'If there aren't any such things as talking dogs, what are you?'

'She's got me there,' Selby thought. 'What can I tell her? Hmmm, I think it's time to stop selling and start running!'

'Now that's an interesting question and I think you'll love the answer,' Selby said, suddenly bolting and heading for a bush.

'Not so fast!' Harold Huckster said, grabbing one of Selby's legs and then grabbing another leg.

Selby was still trying to run when Mrs Huckster grabbed his other two legs.

'Good grief!' Selby thought. 'I've run out of legs again! They've got me!'

But before Selby could think of what to do next, the Trifles' car pulled up and Mrs Trifle jumped out.

'What are you doing to our dog?' she cried, snatching Selby away from them.

'I-I-I'm afraid our car hit him,' Harold Huckster said. 'He ran in front of us. We didn't have time to stop.'

'We're terribly sorry,' Mrs Huckster said.

'Poor baby,' Mrs Trifle said. 'He seems to be okay but we'd better get him in the house and let him rest.'

'Excuse me,' Harold said. 'But would you sell him to us?'

'Sell him?!' Mrs Trifle exclaimed. 'To you?! Are you kidding?! Do you realise what a special dog he is?'

'W-Well yes, we do,' Mrs Huckster said.

'Then how could you possibly ask a question

like that?' Mrs Trifle demanded. 'There isn't another dog like him in the whole of Australia.'

'And, perhaps, the world,' Dr Trifle added as the Trifles started to walk towards the house.

'Well, no, I guess there isn't,' Harold Huckster said. 'Sorry I asked.'

'As well you should be,' Selby thought. And with this Selby suddenly flashed his super-spectacular ear-to-ear all-over-his-face smile at the baffled Hucksters.

THE PADDLE-PUP

'Goodness me,' Mrs Trifle said as she stopped the car at Bogusville Lake, 'the plants have been delivered but where are the BLURVAC people?'

Selby looked out the car window at the hundreds and hundreds of tiny plastic flower pots, each with a tiny plant in it.

'BLURVAC people?' Dr Trifle asked. 'What are BLURVAC people?'

'It stands for the Bogusville Lake Undergrowth Regeneration Volunteer Action Committee. The volunteers are supposed to be here to help us plant lots of nice native plants around the Bogusville Lake. Don't tell me I told them the wrong day?'

'You must have,' Dr Trifle said, 'otherwise I'm sure they'd be here.'

'I think you're right,' Mrs Trifle sighed. 'Oh,

well, let's get to work. It's very hot and if we aren't quick about it, all the seedlings will die. They're already wilting.'

'I'll be with you in a moment,' Dr Trifle said, lifting a bizarre contraption out of the boot.

'What is that?' Mrs Trifle asked. 'It looks like a horse robot.'

'It's a swimming machine for dogs.'

'But dogs all know how to swim from the moment they're born.'

'All of them except Selby,' Dr Trifle said. 'Selby has never been able to swim a stroke.'

'So you've invented this for Selby, have you?'

'Exactly! We just strap Selby on top of it, put it in the water, turn it on, and off he'll go, dog-paddling away like a normal pooch. It should be a wonderful experience for Selby. He may even get a taste for swimming and then learn how to do it on his own.'

'What do you call it? Did you give it one of those long funny names you think up like a Canine Aquatic Propulsion Simulation Instructing Zoom Equilibrator?'

'Goodness, no,' Dr Trifle said. 'That would spell CAPSIZE. And *capsize* means to tip over and sink. This invention could never tip over —

or sink. Well, I hope not, anyway. I call it my *Paddle-Pup* because it paddles and it's for pups.'

'I wish Dr Trifle would just let me be a happy not-normal non-dog-paddling dog,' Selby thought. 'Besides, I don't trust that Paddle-Pup thing. Something always goes wrong with his inventions. In fact, if he tries to put me on it I'll have to bark and growl and bare my teeth till he has to let me go.'

Dr Trifle lifted Selby onto the invention and began strapping his legs to its mechanical legs.

'Now it's time to bark and growl and bare my teeth,' Selby thought. 'But I can't bring myself to do it. The Trifles are such wonderful people. They're always so good to me. They never even raise their voices at me. How can I be nasty to them? Oh, well, I may as well go along with this Paddle-Pup business. I only hope the flamin' thing floats.'

Dr Trifle carried the invention into the water with Selby on it.

'Phew! It does float,' Selby thought. 'Hey, this is okay. And the water feels great — it's so lovely and cool on my legs.'

Dr Trifle reached down under the water and switched the machine on. Suddenly all four legs began making short sharp dog-paddling strokes. In a minute Selby was moving slowly through the water.

'This is great!' Selby thought as the Paddle-Pup made its way out towards the middle of the lake. 'It's slow, but that's okay with me.'

'Aren't you afraid that the Paddle-Pup will get away?' Mrs Trifle said, bending down and chipping a hole into the hard earth with her garden trowel.

'It's a tiny lake,' Dr Trifle said. 'Where could it go?'

'What if it suddenly stops? What if the battery conks out?'

'I'd just swim out and pull him to shore. You worry too much — Selby's perfectly safe.'

For the next half hour Selby sat on the machine as it paddled around slowly. He quickly learned that he could lean to make the Paddle-Pup turn.

On the shore nearby he watched the Trifles struggling to dig holes in the rock-hard ground. The sweat poured off them and every now and then they groaned and straightened up, stretching their sore backs and stiff legs.

'They'll never get all of those plants in the

ground in time,' Selby thought. 'It's such slow work. Hmmm, speaking of slow, I'm getting a bit tired of piddle-paddling around at low speed on this Paddle-Pup. I wonder if I can crank it up a bit? There must be a speed thingy somewhere — but where would it be? Maybe it's underwater.'

Selby held his breath, put his head underwater, and then opened his eyes.

'There it is,' he thought as he managed to work one paw out of its strap. He pulled the speed lever back with his paw and felt the Paddle-Pup speed up. 'Wow! Suddenly I don't feel like a dog anymore — I'm a one-dog speed boat! I'm a canine cabin cruiser! *Wheeeeeeeeeeeeee*! This is fantastic!'

The Trifles looked on in horror as Selby began tearing around the lake. First he went straight towards them and then he leaned to one side and the Paddle-Pup turned at the last minute and went around in circles.

'Look, I can even do a figure eight!' Selby thought. 'Which is really just the S in Selby only connected up. Maybe I can do one of those loopy loop things like I've seen on that TV channel.'

Selby leaned this way and that as he tore around and around the little lake.

'Ooops! The Trifles will think the Paddle-Pup's out of control,' he thought. 'I'd better slow down again before I give them heart attacks.'

Selby put his paw on the speed lever to push it forward again and slow the Paddle-Pup down but the force of the moving water pushed his paw back in the other direction.

'Uh-oh! The faster it goes, the faster the water makes it go! I can't slow down! I can only speed up! Help!'

Now Selby was going around so fast that his waves were crashing on the shore.

'I can't do this any longer,' he screamed in his brain. 'This dog-paddling dodo could explode! My only chance is to run it up on the shore! Here goes!'

Selby tore out of the water and right past the terrified Trifles, the little metal legs of the Paddle-Pup pounding away at the hard ground like four jackhammers.

'This thing is even faster on land than it is in the water!' Selby thought. 'It's not stopping! I've got to grab the speed lever and push it forward.'

Selby reached for the speed lever but now the

machine bounced and bobbed and jumped and rattled so furiously that he couldn't keep his paw still.

'I can't grab it!'

Around and around the shore Selby tore, sending Dr and Mrs Trifle diving into the water to get out of his way. He sped uphill and downhill and even round-and-round hill, through trees and bushes.

'Help me, please!' Selby screamed out loud. 'This runaway robot's going to kill me! *Heeeeeeeeeeeeelp*!'

Suddenly the Paddle-Pup tore over a hump and straight into a clump of thick bushes where it came to a sudden stop.

'What a strange noise the engine was making there at the end,' Dr Trifle said as he and Mrs Trifle ran out of the water. 'It sounded like a person calling for help.'

'Never mind about that. Thank goodness the battery finally ran out of electricity,' Mrs Trifle said, cuddling the trembling dog. 'Poor baby. You must have had a terrible fright. It's a horrible nasty awful invention, isn't it?'

'Are you kidding?!' Dr Trifle exclaimed as he looked back towards the lake. 'This horrible invention isn't so horrible after all. It just saved us a lot of work.'

'What do you mean?'

'Look at all those neat little holes it made in the ground. They're perfect to put the plants in. Selby did most of our work for us in just a few seconds.'

'Why so he did. Good boy, Selby,' Mrs Trifle said, releasing the straps and letting Selby climb off the machine.

'There's only one problem,' Dr Trifle said.

'And what might that be?'

'There still aren't enough holes. We need about fifty more,' Dr Trifle explained. 'We could do them ourselves but the Paddle-Pup could do them more quickly.'

'What are we going to do?' Mrs Trifle asked. 'The Paddle-Pup's battery is flat.'

'Thank goodness for that,' Selby thought.

'I've got a brilliant idea!' Dr Trifle said, snapping his fingers the way he did when he got brilliant ideas. 'We'll use the spare battery from the car! Quick, grab Selby and strap him on again. We can run him around the shore a couple more times.'

'Not on your life!' Selby thought. 'I'm not

going back on that rattle trap for all the plants in the world!'

'Goodness!' Mrs Trifle cried. 'What's got into him? He's barking and growling and baring his teeth at us! I've never seen him act like this before.'

'I'm sorry,' Selby thought as he jumped free and broke into a run, 'but there are times when even a faithful loving dog just has to say no. If they want that maniac metal monster to punch some more holes then they can ride it themselves!'

SELBY'S SURPRISE

'Do you remember my clever little two-part plan?' Mrs Trifle asked Dr Trifle.

'Plan? Who, me?' said Dr Trifle as he looked up from his workbench.

'You know, the one about Jetty's birthday.'

'Oh, *that* clever little two-part plan. No, I've completely forgotten.'

'Today's her birthday and part one of the plan is me taking her out to a restaurant. Billy is away on a camp but Willy will be coming here if you don't mind looking after him.'

'Will he?' Dr Trifle asked looking back at his latest invention.

'Yes, Willy. Are you going deaf or something?'

'No, I said "will *he*?", not *Willy*. Will he be coming to stay?'

'Just for the night. Is that okay with you?'

'I don't mind but the last time he was here he used some disgraceful language. I warned him once but when it happened again, I had to give him a good spanking. Also, I don't like the way he treats Selby. He can be rather rough, you know.'

'Jetty says that he's not like that anymore. She says he's grown up a lot recently. He doesn't use naughty words and I'm sure he'll be good to Selby.'

'Grown up, schmown up,' Selby thought. 'That little monster won't be grown up when he's ninety! He may grow taller but he'll never ever grow *up*!'

'I don't mind looking after him if he behaves himself,' Dr Trifle said.

'Good. Now I'd better get to work on part two of my clever little plan. I've got a lot of Jetty's friends to ring.'

'And I'm outta here,' Selby thought as he crept out to the backyard and crawled into his favourite hiding bush.

Selby lay there in the dark.

'I can't keep from thinking terrible thoughts about Willy. I know it's not nice — but I can't help myself.'

Just then Selby heard Aunt Jetty's voice. A few

minutes later he heard the two women drive away and there was a terrifying stillness in the air.

'I don't like this,' Selby thought. 'It's too quiet. It's like the calm before the storm. I know that kid is around here somewhere and I know he'll be after me. I wonder what he's up to?'

Suddenly Selby heard the crackle of breaking branches and there was Willy only a leg's length away. Selby got ready to run.

'Don't run away,' Willy pleaded. 'I won't hurt you. Please, I wanna be your friend.'

'Friend?' Selby thought. 'Did he say friend? Who is this kid trying to kid?'

'I won't hurt you anymore. Shake hands with Willy. I know you can talk but I won't tell nobody. Come on, doggy. Be my friend.'

'This has got to be a trick,' Selby thought, looking around for hidden cameras or tape recorders that would catch him talking.

'Please,' Willy said putting his hand out further.

'Back off, brat!' Selby whispered. 'One step closer and I'm out of here and over the back fence. You won't see me again!'

Willy pulled his hand back. Selby could see tears forming in the boy's eyes.

'Don't be mean to me,' Willy whimpered.

'What's wrong with this kid?' Selby wondered. 'I've never seen anything like it. Suddenly the monster has turned to mush.'

'I'm sorry,' the boy blubbered.

'What are you up to?' Selby asked out loud. 'What's your game this time?'

'Do you want to play a game?' Willy asked.

'No, I mean what's your angle? What's your pitch? You're trying to trap me into giving away my secret gift of the gab — I know you are.'

'No, no, cross my heart,' Willy said crossing his heart with his finger. 'I'm not gonna be bad to you.'

'Why don't I believe you?' Selby said.

'It's true,' Willy whined. 'I'll be good.'

Selby could hear Dr Trifle's footsteps approaching.

'Willy?' Dr Trifle said. 'Didn't I warn you not to lay a hand on Selby?'

'I'm not doing anything,' Willy said, bursting into tears again. 'I'm not gonna hurt him, honest. He's a good little doggy.'

'Yes, he is,' Dr Trifle said. 'What's wrong, Willy? Why are you crying?'

'I'm not gonna be bad!' Willy burst out.

'Okay, Willy. Would you like a nice cool drink?'

'No thank you, Dr Trifle,' Willy sniffled.

'Suit yourself, Willy. Now I'd better go and make dinner.'

Selby watched as Dr Trifle went back into the house.

'See?' Willy said. 'I didn't tell him you can talk. I didn't tell him your secret or anything.'

'No, you didn't,' Selby admitted. 'Of course he wouldn't have believed you — but that's never stopped you in the past.'

'Shake hands and we'll be friends,' Willy said, putting out his hand.

'You're going to grab me, aren't you?' Selby said. 'You've got a trick up your sleeve.'

Willy began to cry again so Selby reached out slowly and let Willy shake his paw. Then Selby pulled his paw back.

'Maybe Willy *has* grown up,' he thought.

'Now we're friends,' Willy said.

'So you're not going to call me names anymore?'

'Names? What names?'

'Let's see now, I think I remember "poo-poo stink-face doggy". And then there was —'

'No! No more names,' Willy interrupted.

'Okay, I'll try to forget about the past,' Selby said. 'It won't be easy but I'll work on it.'

'Can I just sit here with you?' Willy asked, wiping his eyes.

'Sure, why not?' Selby sighed. 'But this is the strangest thing that's ever happened to me. I don't know what to think. Suddenly the whole world seems like a different place — a nicer place. It's going to take some getting used to.'

'Whaddaya mean?'

'Never mind, kid. I'll explain it when you're older.'

And so it was that Selby and Willy sat in the darkness talking and talking until the stars came out. When Dr Trifle called, Willy went inside to eat dinner but then he came back for more talk. Finally Dr Trifle called him again.

'Willy? Time for bed.'

'Okay, Dr Trifle, coming.'

But once again Willy burst into tears.

'Now what's wrong?' Selby asked.

'I forgot Selby,' Willy whimpered.

'What do you mean, you forgot me? I'm right here.'

'No, my teddy Selby.'

'Your teddy bear is named Selby?'

'Yes, I named him after you.'

'Oh, that's sweet,' Selby said.

'But I left him at home,' Willy said. 'And now I won't be able to sleep. I need my teddy or I can't sleep.'

'Maybe you could ask Dr Trifle to pop over to your house and pick him up for you?'

'No. He's too busy. I don't want to ask him.'

'Well that's very considerate of you,' Selby said.

'He's right on the floor in my bedroom,' Willy said looking at Selby with big wide teary eyes.

'Hang on, kid. If you think I'm going to go over there to get your teddy then you've got another think coming.'

'Please,' Willy pleaded. 'Nobody's at home.'

'I know,' Selby said. 'Your brother's away and your mother's in a restaurant with Mrs Trifle. But I'm still not going.'

'The door is open. You just go in.'

'No way, Willy! I'm glad we're friends now but this is asking too much.'

'You were mean to me, too,' Willy reminded him. 'You did lots of mean things.'

'Only because you deserved it. I never ever started it.'

'Okay,' Willy sniffed. 'Goodnight, Selby.'

Selby watched as Willy went back into the house.

'I do feel sorry for the kid,' Selby admitted. 'He really has grown up — and he wants to be my friend. It must have taken a lot of guts to come right out and say it.'

Selby lay there as a light rain began to fall.

'This is awful,' he thought. 'Now I feel guilty about being nasty to Willy. It's true that I did get him into heaps of trouble. Maybe I should go and get his teddy bear for him. If I don't the poor kid will probably lie awake all night.'

It began to rain harder and, just as Selby was about to go indoors, he made the decision.

'Okay, so I'll pop over to his house and get the teddy bear. It'll only take a few minutes. I'll take some shortcuts through people's yards so Mrs Trifle won't see me on the road if she's driving home.'

Selby climbed over the back fence and dashed from yard to yard and down two back lanes towards Aunt Jetty's house, splashing his way through mud puddles along the way.

'Yuck,' he muttered. 'I'm going to be filthy by the time I get there.'

Minutes later Selby found himself in front of Aunt Jetty's house. He walked quietly down the path, wiped the mud off his feet on the doormat and got ready to go in.

'Good. Mrs Trifle hasn't brought her home yet,' he thought as he looked at the darkened house. 'Well, here goes. I only hope I can find that teddy bear in the dark because I'm not going to risk turning on lights.'

Selby reached up, turned the handle slowly with two paws and opened the door very quietly before slipping inside.

'I'll just stand here a minute till my eyes get used to the dark,' he said out loud. 'Hmmm, I wonder where that bedroom is.'

Suddenly Selby sensed something strange. As his eyes adjusted to the dark he saw shapes around him moving slightly. Then suddenly the lights went on and Selby was surrounded by people wearing paper party hats and throwing streamers.

'Surprise! Surprise! Happy birthday!' they all cheered and then they suddenly went silent at the sight of Selby.

Selby froze.

'Oh, no!' he screamed in his brain. 'I've

walked into a surprise birthday party for Aunt Jetty! That was the "part two" that Mrs Trifle was talking about and the reason for all those phone calls! Mrs Trifle took her to a restaurant and then she must be going to bring her back here to be surprised! That little brat Willy knew this! He set me up! Now everyone's seen me opening a door and they even heard me talk! Now they know I'm not just an ordinary non-talking non-door-opening dog! What am I going to do? Oh well, when in doubt *run for it*!'

Selby was about to turn and run when suddenly he saw Mrs Trifle and Aunt Jetty coming down the path behind him.

'Out of my way!' he screamed into the room full of shocked faces and ran into the house and into a back bedroom. There his foot hit something and he fell flat on his face.

'Willy's teddy bear! Just my luck I'd trip over the flamin' thing! Okay, if that brat wants it back, he's going to get it back. But I don't think he's going to be very happy.'

In a second he was up and struggling to open the back window.

'What's going on here?!' he heard Mrs Trifle ask from the other room. 'You weren't supposed to turn the lights on till we got here. Now it's not a surprise.'

'B-B-But there was this dog!' someone said. 'And he talked!'

'Talked? What do you mean, *talked*?'

'Like *talk* talked. He opened his mouth and words came out! Honest!' another voice said.

'What did this talking dog look like?' Mrs Trifle asked as Selby still struggled with the stuck window in the bedroom.

'He looked like your dog, Mayor Trifle. But he couldn't have been because he was dark brown! He's in the bedroom. Have a look for yourself!'

Selby heard the sound of running feet but before they came into the room, the window finally flew open. He hit the ground running and in a second was over the back fence and heading for home.

'Brown? Why did they think I was dark brown?' Selby thought. 'Oh, I get it — it's the mud! I'm covered in mud! Thank goodness for that!'

Selby washed himself with the garden hose before sneaking back into the Trifles' house through the hole in the back of the garage. There, waiting for him, was Willy, wearing green pyjamas and a great wide gleeful grin.

'They caught you, didn't they, you poop-head?!' Willy squealed.

'Almost, Willy,' Selby said, dropping the teddy bear at his feet. 'But not quite. Better luck next time, you little scoundrel.'

Willy looked down at the teddy bear.

'Look what you did to Teddy!' he screamed.

'Oh, so his name isn't Selby, after all.'

'He's all chewed! You did that on purpose!'

'Oh did I?' Selby said, clutching the bear in his paws and then ripping its head off with his teeth. 'I'm sooooo sorry.'

'Why you stupy-stinky-poopy dog!' Willy bawled, grabbing Selby by the throat and shaking him violently.

Just then Dr Trifle barged though the door and stood watching in horror.

'What do you think you're doing?!' Dr Trifle demanded, pulling Willy away from Selby. 'I warned you not to use that sort of language and not to lay a hand on Selby! Now I'm going to lay a hand on you!'

'He talks!' Willy cried. 'He knows how to talk. Honest, he does!'

Selby looked up innocently as Dr Trifle put Willy across his knee.

It was a calm and collected Selby who slunk silently away to get a good night's sleep. Soon he could hear the soothing sound of Willy's screams as Dr Trifle beat time on his bottom.

'There are times when I really do feel sorry for that brat,' Selby yawned. 'But I don't think this is one of them.'

SELBY HOUSE BOUND

'Selby, fetch!' Dr Trifle called, throwing a stick. 'Come on, boy, bring it back to me.'

'He's got to be joking,' Selby thought. 'My stick-chasing days are over. It's *sooooo* dumb. He throws the stick and I bring it back. Then he throws it again and I bring it back again. It's just not something for a thinking, feeling, reading and writing dog like me to be doing.'

'What's wrong with Selby?' Dr Trifle asked, throwing another stick onto a growing pile of sticks. 'He used to fetch sticks but he doesn't anymore.'

'I used to do it to make him feel happy,' Selby thought. 'But now it bores me out of my brain.'

'Maybe he's forgotten what to do,' Mrs Trifle said.

'Is that possible?' Dr Trifle said. 'Do you

suppose he's just getting old and his memory is going?'

'With Selby, anything is possible. But never mind. We have something else we have to do: we're going to buy a house.'

'Buy a house? But we already have a house.'

'We have a *little* house. This is a nice *big* house.'

'I never knew that you wanted to live in a bigger house.'

'Yes, one that doesn't have lots of other houses all around it — where it'll be peaceful and quiet.'

'And you've actually found a house like that?' Dr Trifle said, throwing another stick onto the pile.

'Yes, it's right out in the country. It's where that old mine used to be, in Slaghaven Heights. I rang the real-estate agent and she'll be meeting us at the house shortly.'

'Well I suppose it can't do any harm to have a look at it,' Dr Trifle said.

'What's wrong with staying here?' Selby thought. 'I love this house. I hope Mrs Trifle isn't serious about moving.'

Twenty minutes later Elvira Poshbody, the real-estate agent, met the Trifles and Selby in front of the empty house. It had just begun to rain.

'This is the most fabulous house,' Mrs Poshbody said. 'I just know you're going to love it.'

'It looks okay,' thought Selby, 'but that's not the point: living way out here would give me the creeps. Besides, I like where we live now. It's only a short walk to town. I could never get to town from here unless someone drove me. I hope it's horrible inside.'

'Do show us through it,' Mrs Trifle said. 'It does look quite stunning.'

'Yes, I'm impressed too,' Dr Trifle said.

'That's the last thing I wanted to hear,' Selby thought. 'Maybe there's some way that I can put them off it. I'll have to think of something.'

When Mrs Poshbody opened the door, Selby went ahead of them through the first room and into the next room.

'Bad luck: the house looks okay,' he thought. 'Maybe I could do something to make it look not so okay . . .'

Selby suddenly spied a pencil lying on the floor.

'I'll try the old cracked walls trick,' he thought. 'That'll give them something to think about.'

Selby drew some jagged lines on the wall and then quickly dropped the pencil again as the real-estate agent led the Trifles into the room.

'Look at this magnificent dining-room,' the woman said. 'Can't you just see yourself and ten of your closest friends sitting here on a warm summer's day eating and talking?'

'It is nice,' said Mrs Trifle. 'But tell me this: is the house sinking?'

'Sinking? Goodness no. These foundations are as solid as old cheese.'

'Then why are there cracks in the walls?' Mrs Trifle asked. 'I think the foundations must be breaking up or sinking — or both.'

'Good point,' Dr Trifle added. 'We wouldn't want to buy a house that had problems like that.'

'Very strange,' Mrs Poshbody said as she looked closely at the walls. 'Goodness me! Look! They aren't cracks at all. They're only pencil lines made to look like cracks. Someone's been scribbling on the walls.'

'Why so they have,' Dr Trifle laughed. 'Isn't that strange?'

'Crumbs,' Selby thought. 'I guess I'll have to do better than that.'

Selby raced around through another room and into the kitchen ahead of the group.

'Hmmm, it's raining now,' he thought. 'What a good time for the old leaky roof trick. Maybe they won't want to buy the house if the roof leaks.'

With this he quietly got some water from the sink and poured a big puddle on the floor.

'Now I'd better hide,' Selby thought as he climbed into the cupboard under the sink, 'or they'll think it's a Selby puddle and not a leaking roof puddle.'

Just as Selby closed the cupboard door Mrs Poshbody led the Trifles into the kitchen.

'And here is your dream kitchen,' the woman said. 'Just think of the fabulous meals you'll be able to make here. Good food makes a happy home.'

'It's very nice,' Mrs Trifle said. 'But tell me something: does the roof leak?'

'Roof? Leak? Impossible!' Mrs Poshbody exclaimed, waving her hands in the air. 'Why this house has the tightest, driest roof in the whole of Slaghaven Heights.'

'Then how do you explain this puddle?' Mrs Trifle said, pointing.

'Oh, that! I-I-I . . .' Mrs Poshbody said, suddenly at a loss for words. 'I spilled a glass of water just before you arrived, that's what I did. And I didn't have time to wipe it up.'

'Hang on a tick!' Selby thought. '*She* didn't spill any water — *I* did! She's not telling the truth. Okay, so I was, well, slightly sneaky when I drew those pencil marks and slightly sneaky again when I poured the water on the floor but she doesn't know that. She must *think* that the roof really is leaking and now she's lying to the Trifles!'

'Well that's a relief,' Mrs Trifle said. 'You had me worried for a minute there.'

'What's the plumbing like?' Dr Trifle asked.

'Of course it's an old house, as you can see,' Mrs Poshbody said, 'but the plumbing is all brand spanking new.'

'Brand spanking nothing,' Selby said, looking at the pipes next to his head. 'These pipes are so old that only the rust is holding them together. There she goes, lying again! No more Mr Nice Dog. No more Mr Slightly-Sneaky Dog either. Now she's going to learn what a down-and-dirty dog can do!'

'Have a look how beautifully the water flows out of these lovely taps,' Mrs Poshbody said, reaching to turn on the water.

'We'll see about that,' Selby thought.

The moment he heard the agent turn the water on, Selby began banging a pot against a water pipe.

'What's that?' Dr Trifle asked. 'The plumbing must be wonky if it makes that banging noise every time you turn on the taps.'

'Banging noise?' Mrs Poshbody asked, quickly turning off the water. Selby stopped banging. 'What banging noise?' the woman added.

She turned the water on again and this time Selby banged even harder.

'*That* banging noise,' Mrs Trifle said.

'Oh, *that* banging noise. That's — well — that's —'

'Wonky plumbing,' Mrs Trifle cut in.

'No, no, it's the latest thing in plumbing. It's a special feature that makes sure you don't leave the water running by mistake. That's what it is. Yes. You see, the banging reminds you to turn it off.'

'What a clever invention,' said Dr Trifle. 'I wish I'd thought of it first.'

'Crumbs,' Selby thought. 'The problem with the Trifles is that they're too trusting. They're so honest that they think that everyone else is honest too. I've got to protect them from this awful woman! This calls for the old faulty wiring trick.'

From where Selby was hiding no one could see the paw that reached up and switched the lights quickly off and on.

'Goodness!' Dr Trifle said. 'There's something wrong with the wiring.'

'I beg your pardon?' the woman said.

'The wiring,' Mrs Trifle sighed. 'There must be a short-circuit somewhere which is making the lights flicker. Why the whole house could catch fire.'

'No, no, that's not true. This house could never burn down,' the real-estate agent said. 'That flickering is a new service from the electricity company.'

'A new service?' Dr Trifle said. 'Who would want their lights flickering all day?'

'It doesn't happen every day. They do it to tell you when it's time to pay the bill. You just phone them and they tell you how much you owe. That way they don't have to send you a notice or anything. It saves time and it saves postage and think of all the trees they don't have to cut down to make paper to print all those electricity bills. It is very good for the environment.'

'Another brilliant idea,' Dr Trifle said. 'There are people out there thinking all the time.'

'Now follow me, there's lots more to see,' the real-estate agent said, leading the Trifles out of the kitchen.

'Well, the cracks trick and the puddle trick and the noisy pipes and faulty wiring tricks didn't work — at least this cunning little dog still has one last card up his sleeve,' Selby thought as he crept up the back stairs and then climbed through the hole that went into the roof. 'I saw a program on TV recently about rats getting into roofs. I'll give them the old rats in the roof trick.'

With this he scampered lightly back and forth across the ceiling.

'Bush rats!' he heard Dr Trifle say. 'The roof is full of rats! There could be hundreds of them. I saw a program on TV recently about rats getting into roofs. They're lovely little creatures but when they make nests in your house, they can do terrible damage. And they're so hard to get rid of. No matter what you do they just keep coming back.'

'They're not rats,' the real-estate agent said. 'What you hear is the gentle sound of gumnuts bumping together in the breeze in that beautiful old gum tree just outside the window.'

'Bumping gumnuts?' Dr Trifle said. 'Well that's no problem. In fact I kind of like the sound of that.'

'Me too,' Mrs Trifle said. 'I think I'm going to like living close to nature.'

'I give up,' Selby thought as he crept back downstairs. 'That woman is too smart for me. I guess I'll just have to get used to living way out here. Oh, well.'

Selby sighed a deep sigh and sat down next to the Trifles.

'Now if you'll just sign the contract, the house will be yours,' the woman said.

'Do you mean you want us to buy the house right now?' Dr Trifle asked.

'Why yes.'

'But this is all so sudden,' Mrs Trifle said. 'Could we just think it over for a few days?'

'Think it over? Are you kidding? Do you realise that there are sixteen other people waiting to get their hands on this prime piece of property?'

'Sixteen? Really?' Dr Trifle asked.

'Well at least twelve. Six of them wanted to sign the contract this morning but I said no — I'm giving the Trifles the first go at it,' the woman said. 'And do you know why I'm doing this for you?'

'No, why?' Mrs Trifle asked.

Mrs Poshbody put her hand on Mrs Trifle's arm and then smiled warmly.

'Because I like you,' she said. 'I like you both enormously. You're such wonderful lovely people.'

'Really?' Mrs Trifle said with a blush. 'Oh, well, I guess we've decided to buy the house, haven't we, dear?'

'Yes, I think we have,' Dr Trifle said.

'Oh, that woman is a smarmy charmy little liar!' Selby thought. 'She's just saying that to get the trusting Trifles to buy the house before they have a chance to think it over.'

Seconds later the contract was signed.

'You are now the proud owners of the best house in Tipperary Road, Slaghaven Heights,' the real-estate agent said. 'In fact it's the *only* house in Tipperary Road.'

'Tipperary Road?' Mrs Trifle said. 'Where have I heard that name before?'

'Tipperary,' Dr Trifle said very slowly. 'That does sound familiar. Tip — Tip — Tip —'

'Tip!' Mrs Trifle cried. 'That's it! Tipperary Road is where they're going to put the new rubbish tip! I completely forgot! It'll be right next to the house!'

'Well, yes, but I'm sure it won't be that bad,' Mrs Poshbody said with a smile.

'Why didn't you warn us? We don't want to live next to a rubbish tip.'

'Because you didn't ask,' Mrs Poshbody said, rubbing her hands together. 'Besides, it'll be so easy to get rid of your rubbish — all you'll have to do is throw it out the window!' she added with a laugh.

'We've just changed our minds,' Dr Trifle said. 'We don't want to buy the house after all.'

'Sorry — it's too late,' Mrs Poshbody sang, heading for the door with the contract in her hands. 'You signed the contract so it's too bad for you — as long as you have the contract you have to buy the house.'

'This is awful!' Selby thought. 'I can't let this happen to my dear sweet owners, the Trifles. Besides, I don't want to live next to a tip either!'

'You cheated us!' Mrs Trifle cried. 'You wretch!'

Suddenly something in Selby snapped. Before he knew it, he'd leapt high in the air, snatched the contract from Mrs Poshbody's hands, and was tearing it to shreds.

'Give me that, you awful dog!' the woman screamed. 'Make him give it to me, Mrs Trifle.'

'Make him give what to you?' Mrs Trifle said

as Selby dropped what was left of the contract at her feet.

'Your dog destroyed a legal contract! He could go to jail for that! Now you have to sign another one!'

'Oh, really?' Mrs Trifle said. 'What is this woman talking about?'

'Contract? Jail?' Dr Trifle said. 'I have no idea. I think she's gone gaga.'

'Well!' the woman exclaimed.

She turned on her heels, strode out of the house, and drove away.

'Thank goodness for Selby,' Mrs Trifle said.

'Yes,' Dr Trifle said. 'It was almost as if he knew what was happening. You don't suppose he really understands what we're saying, do you?'

'Don't be silly, dear.'

'Well when he grabbed that contract it did seem like he was trying to protect us from our own mistake.'

'No, no,' Mrs Trifle said. 'He must have grabbed the contract because I called that woman a *wretch*.'

'That's what I mean: he understood what you were saying.'

'It's not that — he thought I said *fetch*. When

72

he heard *fetch* he grabbed the contract and brought it back to me.'

'I see!' said Dr Trifle. 'And that means that his memory's come back. I'd better throw some sticks for him before he forgets again.'

'Crumbs,' Selby thought. 'Now I'm going to have to spend the rest of the day watching Dr Trifle throw sticks. It's not fair! It seems that every time I win — I lose!'

Dr Trifle's War of Words

'*Varoooooooom,*' said Dr Trifle.

'*Varoom?*' asked Mrs Trifle as she tried to start the car for the second time.

'No, *varoooooooom!*' Dr Trifle said again. 'With lots of *ooooom* in it.'

'*Varoooooooom!*'

'That's better.'

'What kind of word is *varoooooooom?*' Mrs Trifle asked as she tried to start the car for the third time.

'It means *car,*' Dr Trifle answered.

'In what language?'

'In *Blabble-dabble.*'

'I beg your pardon?'

'Blabble-dabble. That's what I call my new language. I'm going to make up all new words for everything.'

'Why make up words? There are already too many of them, if you ask me.'

'I agree,' Selby thought as he sat on the back seat listening to the Trifles. 'We should be getting rid of words, not making up new ones.'

'Most words are silly,' Dr Trifle said, watching as Mrs Trifle once again tried to start the car. 'Take the word *car*, for example.'

'*Car*?' Mrs Trifle said. 'What's so silly about *car*?'

'It's just a sound,' Dr Trifle explained. 'It doesn't have any real meaning.'

'It means a great chunk of metal that whizzes around the roads going varooom varooom —'

'Which is exactly why it should be called a *varoooooooom*!' Dr Trifle interrupted. 'The word *car* just doesn't sound right. Just say it a few times.'

'*Car car car car car car*,' Mrs Trifle said very quickly.

'You see? You sound like a crow. Come to think of it, that's brilliant! *Car* will be my new Blabble-dabble name for *crow*,' Dr Trifle said getting out a notepad and writing the word *car* very neatly.

'I just wish this car would start,' Selby thought.

75

'I was kind of looking forward to a trip to the supermarket. I don't want to sit here much longer, this Blabble-dabble stuff is straining my brain.'

'Don't you see,' Dr Trifle said, putting on his serious explaining voice, 'words should make us think of the things they are. That way we wouldn't need dictionaries.'

'But I just bought a dictionary,' Mrs Trifle said.

'Throw it away. We won't need it. In a little while everyone will be speaking Blabble-dabble.'

'Do you really expect everyone in the whole world to start talking in your made-up language?'

'Why not?' Dr Trifle asked. 'It will make everything so easy. Then anyone can go to any country and just say *varooooooooom* and people will know that they mean *car*.'

'And if they say *car* everyone will know they mean crow,' Mrs Trifle said.

'Precisely. And there won't be any wars because people will all know exactly what everyone is talking about.'

'Are you sure that people start wars because they have different words for *car*?'

'Wars start when people don't understand each other,' Dr Trifle said. 'If we all used the same words there would be no misunderstandings and no wars. Don't you see what I'm driving at?'

'For the moment we're not driving anywhere. This car — this *varoooooooooom* — doesn't want to start.'

'That's because the *sparkjar* needs *gazapping*,' Dr Trifle explained.

'I beg your pardon?'

'*Sparkjar* is Blabble-dabble for battery. *Gazapping* means putting more electricity in it: recharging it. It's as flat as a tack.'

'I guess we'll have to walk to the supermarket,' Mrs Trifle said. 'I'd better put on my walking shoes —'

'You mean your *shuffle shunks*,' Dr Trifle said.

'If you insist,' Mrs Trifle sighed. 'You ring the Wingnut Brothers' Garage — I mean make a *rinkle-tinkle* to the *clatter-shop*.'

'There, you see?' Dr Trifle said, grinning from ear to ear. 'You're making up Blabble-dabble words already. See how simple it is?'

Selby followed the Trifles into the house. Mrs Trifle went into the bedroom to change her shoes while Dr Trifle picked up the telephone and dialled the garage.

'This is Dr Trifle,' he said. 'Mrs Trifle and I

will be away shopping but would you please come to our house and *gazap* the *sparkjar* in our *varoooooooom*? When you're finished, leave your bill in the letterbox. We'll pay you later. Thank you.'

'Did they understand your Blabble-dabble?' asked Mrs Trifle as she came out of the bedroom.

'I didn't talk to them,' Dr Trifle said. 'I got their *blabber-box*.'

'You mean, their answering machine?' Mrs Trifle guessed.

'Spot on.'

'Hadn't we better leave a note on the car telling them to recharge the battery just in case they don't understand your message?' Mrs Trifle asked.

'No, no. This is an experiment. If they understand Blabble-dabble then they'll recharge the battery.'

'And if they don't?'

'Then they won't recharge the battery. If the car doesn't start when we get home I'll give the *clatter-shop* another *rinkle-tinkle* and explain.' Dr Trifle looked down at Selby. 'Shall we take the *bow-wow* with us?'

'No, poor old thing,' Mrs Trifle said. 'All that walking will only wear him out.'

'Crumbs,' Selby sighed as he watched the Trifles disappear down the street. 'Here I am stuck at home again. It's not fair! Oh well, at least I can watch the Wingnut brothers work on the car. That should be fun.'

No sooner was this thought out of his brain than a tow truck pulled up and Neville and Norville Wingnut jumped out. Selby dashed outside.

'Okay, now it's something about a *sparkjar*,' Norville said to Neville. 'What's a *sparkjar*, Nev?'

'I don't know, Norv. I thought you knew.'

'Well, I don't, Nev. Let's see now, it can't be one of the well-known parts like the air filter or the battery because I know all of them. It must be one of those little parts all the way in the middle of the engine. I always forget their names. I guess we'll have to take the whole car to bits, Nev.'

'How will we know when we've found the *sparkjar*, Norv?'

'It'll be broken, dummy.'

'Then what do we do, Norv?'

'We *gazap* it, Nev. That's what Dr Trifle wants.'

'What's *gazapping*, Norv?'

'I don't know, Nev, let's just find the *sparkjar* first. Then we'll worry about what to do with it.'

'But, Norv, what if we don't find anything

that's broken and needs to be *gazapped*?'

'Then we'll just have to put the car back together again, Nev. That'll be okay because we'll charge Dr Trifle oodles and oodles of money for all the time we spent trying to find this *sparkjar* thingy,' Norville said, rubbing his hands together gleefully. 'And it's his fault anyway, Nev. He should have left us a nice neat note with everything explained in proper words. Come on, Nev, whip a chain around the engine and let's lift it out of there.'

'Oh, no!' Selby thought. 'They're going to take the whole car apart just because of Dr Trifle's silly made-up words!'

For the next two hours Selby watched helplessly as the car became a pile of parts scattered all around the driveway.

'We didn't find anything broken yet, Norv,' Neville said finally. 'I reckon it's time to put it all back together again.'

'No way, Nev. All these parts are made up of parts too.'

'So you reckon we should take the parts apart. Is that it, Norv?'

'That's right, Nev, and it'll mean lots more money for us.'

'This is torture!' Selby thought. 'It's going to cost sooooo much! I've got to do something quick! I've got to tell Neville and Norville that it's only the battery that needs recharging. I think I'll just tell them in plain English. But if I do that they'll know I can talk! My life will be ruined forever! But I have to do it, I just have to.'

Selby was just about to say, 'Excuse me, Nev and Norv, but what Dr Trifle really wanted to say was that the battery is flat,' when suddenly he had a second thought, and then a third thought, and a fourth thought.

'Hang on! Hold the show!' he thought. 'I've got a better idea!'

Selby dashed into the house, scribbled a note and then crept back out again and quietly placed his note on the windscreen. A few minutes later Neville and Norville noticed the note.

'Look at this, Nev,' Norville said.

'What do you think it is, Norv?'

'It's a note, Nev.'

'What kind of a note, Norv?'

'A note note, Nev. It was on the windscreen all the time. Silly us, we didn't even notice it.'

'What does it say, Norv?'

'It says, "Please recharge the battery", Nev.'

'Gosh, Dr Trifle did leave a note after all. What are we going to do now, Norv?'

'There isn't much we can do, Nev. We'd better put the car back together quick smart and recharge the battery before they come home. Better get a wriggle on, Nev, or the Trifles will come home and see how silly we were. Then we'd better get back to the *clatter-shop*.'

'What's a *clatter-shop*, Norv?'

'It's a word I just made up, Nev. I just thought it would be a good word for a garage. Do you like it?'

'It's good, Norv, but I kind of like the old word
— garage. It makes me kind of smile when I say
it. Garage. I guess I don't much like new words
anyway, Norv.'

'Especially ones like *sparkjar*, hey, Nev?'
Norville laughed.

'That's right, Norv.'

Selby had never seen the Wingnut brothers
move so fast. When the Trifles returned, the car
was back together and the Wingnut brothers
were gone. And the car started straight away.

'You see?' Dr Trifle said to Mrs Trifle. 'They
understood my Blabble-dabble perfectly.'

'Why you sneak,' Mrs Trifle said, showing
him the note she'd found. 'You left them a note
just to be on the safe side, didn't you? So much
for your experiment.'

'I didn't. That's not my writing. Look how
messy it is. It's even got the "s" in "please"
written backwards.'

'Hmmm,' Mrs Trifle hmmmed. 'You're right. I
wonder who did write it. It's true that the writing
is far from perfect.'

'All right, all right,' Selby thought. 'So my
writing's not perfect. If they only had paws to
write with their writing would be messy too. At

least the Wingnut brothers knew what the note meant — which is more than I can say for Dr Trifle's Blabble-dabble message. And it saved the Trifles a lot of money. I guess you could say that my writing's not perfect but at least it's *paw*-fect.'

THE DAPPER DOG

It was winter in Bogusville and Selby lay shivering on the lounge reading fashion magazines and looking at the pictures of all the latest fashions.

'These clothes all look so great!' he thought. 'Of course anything would look fantastic with a gorgeous tall and skinny model wearing it. I love that look they always have on their faces. It's sort of like they hate you. Like if you fell down and hurt yourself they'd just step right over you and walk away. It's sort of a I'm-gorgeous-and-you're-not look. But I love it.'

Selby turned a few more pages.

'It's a pity they don't make clothes for dogs,' he thought. 'I could wear all the latest dog fashions. I'd ponce around town and everybody would stop and stare at me and I'd just give

85

them that look. Only I'm not tall and skinny like a model. I wish I was a greyhound.'

Moments later as the Trifles came through the door Selby quickly stuffed the magazines under the lounge.

'I forgot to tell you!' Mrs Trifle exclaimed to Dr Trifle. 'Massimo Panni, the world famous clothing designer, is coming here, to Bogusville, today!'

'Massimo Panni? Here? Why would a world famous designer want to come to Bogusville?'

'I don't know. Probably to get ideas for his fashion designs. I mean we small town people dress so beautifully.'

'We do?'

'Well most of us do,' Mrs Trifle said, putting on a necklace and earrings. 'And guess what? He's not only coming to Bogusville but he's coming right here to this very house.'

'Our house? But he'd be used to going to the fanciest of fancy hotels. He probably lives in a palace. Why would he want to come to our little home?'

'Because I'm the mayor, silly. Important people from overseas always want to meet mayors when they visit a town. So could you please change into a better shirt and trousers?'

'What's wrong with these?'

'Nothing except for the holes in the elbows and knees — and the dirt. You really do look a sight.'

'All right, darling,' Dr Trifle said. 'But they are my most comfortable clothes.'

'Never mind about that. Massimo Panni is a fashion designer and we have to look good for him. Fashion has nothing to do with comfort. Beautiful clothes are always uncomfortable. Why do you think women wear high heels when they dress up?'

'I thought it was to keep their heels dry when they walk through puddles.'

'Don't be silly. They wear them because they're beautiful and because they're uncomfortable. Now slip into your green suit and put on that lovely pink tie. He'll be arriving at any minute.'

'How exciting!' Selby thought. 'Massimo Panni is the greatest! I can't believe this! Oh how I wish I had something beautiful to wear.'

Minutes later four long black cars pulled up in front of the Trifles' house and out stepped the famous designer and twenty-two of his assistants.

'Oooooh, Mrs Mayor!' the designer said, kissing Mrs Trifle's hand. 'This is the first time I come to a country village of Austraaahlia! It is waaanderfool!'

'Thank you, Mr Panni,' Mrs Trifle blushed. 'It's an honour to have you. If there is anything we can do for you, please ask. Would you like a cup of tea? — I mean, twenty-three cups of tea?'

'No, thank you, no. You are too kind.'

'And what brings you to our beautiful town?'

'I come for the inspiration, Mrs Mayor.'

'He gets inspiration *here*?' Selby wondered as he moved closer to get a better look at the great man.

'Yes, yes. Every year I go somewhere for the inspiration. All the time I am in Milano and Paris is no good for me. There is so much fashion there! Fashion, fashion, fashion. I see so many beautiful clothez I go blind! Here is no fashion — nothing! Look at your husband's clothez. A green suit! A pink tie! It is terrible! It is wonderful! I love it!'

'I think it's nice too,' Mrs Trifle said, not knowing quite what to think. 'I gave him the tie for his birthday.'

'Here my eyes are empty. I see no fashion. Then ideas come to Massimo Panni's head. I think of many clothez for my new collection,'

Mr Panni said, patting Selby. 'What is wrong with doggy? He is shaking so much.'

'That's because it's winter,' Mrs Trifle explained. 'He's shivering.'

'Winter is so sad for the animals. They get so cold because they have no clothez. Ahah!' he said, snapping his fingers. 'I have first Massimo Panni brilliant idea of the day! Massimo Panni clothez for the dogs! I make whole collection. I call my collection *Poochi Panni*. Is nice, no? Wonderful brilliant idea of me! Now I have second brilliant idea: I have my doggy fashion show right here!'

'Here? In this town?' Mrs Trifle asked.

'Yes, I make Boringsville very very famous.'

'Excuse me but it's *Bogusville*,' said Mrs Trifle politely correcting the man. 'It sounds very exciting.'

'You will be on TV all around the world! I give everyone big shock!' the designer said, snapping his fingers again. 'I start to drawing my creations now. But wait! Who going to model Poochi Panni doggy clothez?'

'Well I could ring the Bogusville Canine Society and see if anyone can recommend some dog models. I might be able to get some tall thin dogs — some greyhounds, maybe.'

'No, no, no, Mrs Mayor. Why I don't use this doggy to be model for doggy clothez?' the designer said, pointing to Selby. 'I let him be model for girl-dog fashions and boy-dog fashions, too. Makes no difference.'

'Well of course,' Mrs Trifle said. 'I'm sure he'd like that.'

'Oh boy, oh boy, oh boy!' Selby thought. 'I'll be like those models in the magazines! Maybe I *do* have the right looks to be a model, after all. Maybe I *am* gorgeous and just didn't know it!'

'He is perfect!' the designer said. 'Is good to have just boring dog-dog — You know what I say? — People look at clothez and not ugly dog.'

'Hmmm,' thought Selby. 'I'm not sure I agree with that.'

And so it was that for the next two weeks, Massimo Panni and his helpers took over Bogusville Hall and, with a truckload of sewing machines and expensive fabrics, created one fantastic design after another for Selby to wear. By the time the collection was complete Selby had been pricked and scratched by so many pins that he felt like a canine pin-cushion.

Soon everything was ready and Mrs Trifle

chose Farmers' Market Day — when everyone from all around would be in town to do their shopping — for the launch of the 'Poochi Panni Collection'. Bogusville Hall soon filled up with people carrying armloads of groceries.

Also in the hall were the press from all over the world. Some of them even remembered Selby as the Tasmanian Flea-Breeder who helped to catch some international dog-smugglers and the only dog ever to go to Mars. 🐾

'Oh, I'm so scared,' Selby thought as two of Massimo's helpers slipped a yellow chiffon gown covered in tear-drop pearls on him. 'But I love it! I've got to remember to give my best I'm-gorgeous-and-you're-not look. Okay,' he thought, taking a deep breath. 'Here I go out onto the dogwalk.'

The curtain parted and Selby wiggled his way out onto the runway.

'Oh, I'm so nervous,' Selby thought as he took deep breaths to keep his legs from shaking. 'I'm

🐾 *Paw note: See the stories 'Selby Superpooch' and 'Selby Spacedog' in the book* Selby Spacedog *to read about those adventures.* S

gorgeous, I'm gorgeous, I'm gorgeous. I don't believe it but I'll say it again: I'm gorgeous.'

There was a gasp from the crowd and cameras flashed all around.

'They love it!' Selby thought. 'They'll all be buying clothes like these for their dogs! My I'm–gorgeous-and-you're-not look is working perfectly!'

Selby turned on one paw and slunk slowly back behind the curtain. The second he was out of sight he was grabbed by six of Massimo's helpers who whipped off the dress and slipped on a pair of striped shorts, a sports shirt and a pair of sunglasses that fitted him perfectly.

'It's a bit casual,' Selby thought as he slunk back onto the dogwalk. 'But I guess it would be good for dogs who go on holidays with their owners.'

Selby heard groans and giggles all around him.

'I don't think they're so keen on this one,' he thought.

Next Selby found himself in a pin-striped suit with a huge purple hanky poking out of the pocket and a wide-brimmed hat.

'Now this is classy,' Selby thought. 'They're sure to love it.'

Suddenly someone yelled, 'Dax for dogs! I ain't seen nothin' so stupid!'

'It's the purple,' Selby thought. 'Maybe it clashes with my eye colour.'

A ripe tomato flew through the air and smashed against the runway, splattering Selby. Next it was a cabbage and then a dozen eggs landed all around him. Soon the air was filled with flying food.

'Oh, no!' Selby thought. 'What have I done wrong? Maybe I didn't get my I'm-gorgeous-and-you're-not look right. Maybe I smiled and looked friendly by mistake. But never mind that — I've got to get out of here!'

'Come on, let's get outta here!' someone else yelled. 'We've got better things to do than to watch this stupid carry-on!'

Selby bobbed and ducked his way through flying fruit and then skidded on egg-slime until he was safely back behind the curtain.

'Oh, you poor darling,' Mrs Trifle said, helping Selby off with the clothes and giving him a cuddle. 'It wasn't you they were angry at — it was the clothes.'

'They have gone crazies!' the designer cried, peeking out into the emptying hall.

'I think they're just not ready for your designs,' Mrs Trifle said, trying to be as polite as possible.

'Ready for them —? They *hate* them!' the man squealed. 'Everybody in Bulbousville so shocked! Angry! Is so different for them! Is wonderful! Is beautiful! This will be hugest success of Massimo Panni! Thank you, thank you, doggy,' he said, patting Selby.

'But Mr Panni,' Mrs Trifle said, 'why are you so happy?'

'Mrs Mayor, please, you don't understand. Nobody buy my clothez in my shows.'

'They don't?'

'No, no. They too expensive. And they very weird like theez doggy clothez. Nobody want them. But is good everybody get so angry and shock. Now everybody in the world see food-throwing on TV.'

'But why is that good?' Mrs Trifle asked.

'Because now they remember name of Massimo Panni. Then they buy Massimo Panni underpantez. Is good, no?'

'But, Mr Panni, why would anyone want to buy expensive designer underwear when nobody's going to see it?'

'Is true. I don't know why but people buy lots

and lots of Panni Panties and Massimo is very very wealthy man. Goodbye, Mrs Mayor,' he said, kissing her hand. 'Thank you for everything so much.'

'It's been — well — a pleasure, I guess,' Mrs Trifle said. 'Goodbye.'

Selby watched as the designer and his helpers drove away.

'Oh, well,' he thought. 'There goes my last chance to get a decent wardrobe. I guess I'll just have to walk around naked — like every other dog in the world. It doesn't seem fair but what can you do?'

It was winter in Bogusville and Selby lay shivering on the lounge. Only this time instead of reading fashion magazines, he was reading a good book.

SELBY'S STATUE

'So you want me to make a statue of a dog?' the sculptor, Sigfried Slapdash, asked Mrs Trifle when he arrived at Bogusville Town Hall.

'Not just any dog,' Mrs Trifle explained. 'A very famous dog. Her name was Bogus and she was the founder of Bogusville. We want a statue of her to put in Bogusville Park.'

'Excuse me, but did you say that this town was started by a dog? That's absurd. Dogs can't start towns — only people can.'

'Bogus was owned by a man named Brumby Bill about a hundred years ago. He was sick of the city so he moved to the country to look for gold. 🐾

> 🐾 Paw note: For a spooky story about the ghost of Brumby Bill read 'In the Spirit of Things' in the book Selby Speaks. S

One day Bogus wandered away from the campsite and got lost. Brumby Bill finally found her right here. He fell in love with this area, built himself a house, and then he and Bogus just stayed on. Gradually other people moved here and built houses and Brumby Bill named the town Bogusville, after the dog that he loved so much.'

'Oh, isn't that a lovely story,' Selby thought as he lay nearby on the floor, secretly listening.

'So what did this Bogus look like?' the sculptor asked. 'I can't do a sculpture if I don't know what she looked like.'

'We only have this blurry old photo,' Mrs Trifle said, showing him the picture. 'We assume she was part dingo but you can't see her well enough to know. It doesn't really matter. Just make a good sculpture of a normal dog and that will be fine.'

'I've never sculpted a dog before,' the sculptor said getting a huge hunk of wax out of a bag. 'I'll need a model. Otherwise she might come out looking like a cat or a cow or something.'

'I think we have just what you need,' Mrs Trifle said pointing to Selby. 'I brought him along today just in case you needed him. Of course I wouldn't expect you to make your sculpure look *exactly* like Selby.'

'Well, he's a *boy* dog, for starters,' the sculptor said. 'Bogus was a . . . a *girl* dog.'

'Can't you just leave the boy bits off?'

'If that's what you want, sure. You're the mayor of this town so you're the boss.'

'Thank you,' Mrs Trifle said. 'I hoped you'd see it that way.'

'Isn't it great that Bogusville is finally going to have a statue of Bogus!' Selby thought. 'And she's going to have *my* body — only with the boy bits missing, of course.'

'Another thing,' Mrs Trifle said. 'Please don't make the statue look weird.'

'Weird? What do you mean, weird?' Sigfried asked. 'My statues never look weird.'

'Well, yes, but do you remember that statue of the scientist you did? You made his head bigger than the rest of his body.'

'Of course, I remember. That's one of my finest works of art! I gave him a big head to show that he was a great thinker. That's what scientists are all about.'

'Well, we don't want anything like that,' Mrs Trifle said. 'I believe you also sculpted a racehorse with twenty legs.'

'Rubbish!' the sculptor said. 'It was only

sixteen legs. That was to show that the horse was running. That's what racehorses are all about.'

'Well we don't want a sculpture of Bogus with sixteen legs.'

'But sculptures are supposed to make people think,' said Sigfried.

'I'm afraid the people of Bogusville don't like to think very much,' Mrs Trifle said.

'You don't understand. I am an artist. I want my sculptures to *say* something to the people who look at them. I want them to look at my dog sculpture and think: "Now I know something about a dog that I never knew before".'

'You mean they'll learn something? Like what?'

'I don't know yet but I'll think of something.'

'What we want is a statue of a dog that looks like a dog so that when we look at it we think: "Hey, there's a dog!".'

'But that's so boring,' the sculptor protested.

'We can always hire someone else to do the sculpture,' Mrs Trifle reminded him.

'All right,' the sculptor sighed, 'I'll do what you say. If you pay, I'll play. Are you sure this dog can stand still while I do the sculpture?'

'Of course he can, won't you, Selby? He's

very good at standing still. Come to think of it, standing still and lying still are the things he does best,' Mrs Trifle said. 'So how do you make your sculptures?'

'Simple: first I make a model out of wax. Then I cover it all with some glurpy stuff that gets really hard. This is sent off to a foundry where they pour in hot metal and the wax melts and comes out. Then they chip off the outside part and there's the sculpture.'

'That sounds very complicated,' Mrs Trifle said. 'I'll leave you to it. If you need me, I'll be next door in my office.'

After Mrs Trifle had left, Selby sat perfectly still watching Sigfried Slapdash shape the lump of wax with his hands.

'This guy's good!' Selby thought. 'He's got the legs and the tail exactly right. The real test will be the face — my face.'

Selby sat so still that he was beginning to worry about his bottom going to sleep. Then, suddenly, he felt a slight twinge in his ear.

'Crumbs,' he thought. 'I've got a flea in my ear. I just hope he doesn't bite me.'

'Dogs,' Sigfried mumbled. 'I hate dogs. I could never stand them. They're so smelly and bitey and everything. Yuck! Disgusting creatures. But the mayor wants a dog so I guess I have to make a dog. I only wish I could think of what makes dogs so . . . so doglike so that I could put a little bit of art into this sculpture. Hmmm.'

Selby felt the flea crawl out of his ear, move across his forehead and then onto his nose.

'This flea is making me itch — but I've got to keep still,' he thought. 'This sculptor guy is very touchy. If I start moving, he might just pack up and leave and then blame it on me.'

Selby felt the flea crawl around his face as he struggled to stay still. By now there was sweat dripping from his nose.

'It's beginning to look like a dog,' the sculptor muttered. 'But it still isn't telling me anything.'

'I wish he'd just hurry up!' Selby thought. Then suddenly the flea bit him — and then bit him again. 'I can't stand it any longer! I've got to scratch!' Selby thought as he started scratching frantically.

'That's it!' the sculptor cried. 'Dogs are *all about scratching fleas*! When I think of a dog I think of an animal that is always scratching. They are four-legged, foul smelling, scratching machines.'

'Scratching machines?' Selby thought, standing still again. 'What is he talking about? We're not all the same, for starters. We have as many different personalities as people do. Some of us scratch a lot and others don't.'

'I'll make a sculpture of Bogus scratching!' the sculptor said. 'If I'm clever about it I can collect my money and the mayor won't know what I've done until the sculpture comes back from the foundry. By then I'll be long gone. But I'm sure everyone will love my dog.'

Selby watched in horror as Sigfried Slapdash added lots of ears and mouths on the sculpture until the whole face was a mass of eyes and ears and noses.

'Crikey!' Selby thought. 'It's like a moving face in a comic book.'

'A dog scratching a flea! It's perfect!' the sculptor cried.

'It's perfectly horrible!' Selby thought. 'It looks like a mutant dog from outer space!'

'Now to cover it with the mould stuff before the mayor sees it,' the sculptor said.

He quickly mixed up a big bowl of white glurp and spread it all over the statue. Just when he'd finished, Mrs Trifle returned.

'I just popped in to see how you were going,' she said.

'I've finished.'

'Already?'

'They don't call me Slapdash for nothing,' the sculptor said. 'I finished it ages ago. Now all you have to do is wait till this dries and then send the whole thing off to the foundry. They'll pour in the hot metal and then you've got your sculpture.'

'I wish I could have seen it before you put that stuff on it,' Mrs Trifle said.

'You're a very important person and I didn't want to interrupt your work,' the sculptor said. 'Trust me — you'll love it.'

'Oh, well come with me and I'll give you your money.'

'This is awful!' Selby thought when Mrs Trifle and the sculptor had left the room. 'Everyone will hate it! I've got to get that sticky stuff off and fix the face so it looks like a real dog's face.'

Selby dug his claws into the glurp around the sculpture's face and pulled.

'It's already getting hard!' he thought. 'It may be too late!'

Selby put his feet up against the sculpture and

pulled harder until a big soggy chunk flew off, hitting him smack in the face.

'Oh, no!' he thought as he struggled to peel it off his face. 'It's got me! I'm going to suffocate! Help!'

Selby staggered around the room, slowly pulling it off his face until it finally popped free.

'Phew!' he sighed. 'Now to reshape the wax and put some new glurp on it. All I have to do is get rid of some of these eyes, ears and noses. It won't be brilliant but it should be okay.'

Selby was about to press his paws into the wax when he heard footsteps in the corridor.

'Crumbs!' he thought. 'Mrs Trifle is going to catch me! I'd better just whack the glurp back on the face and leave it alone!'

Selby quickly slapped the hardening mould back on the sculpture and then stepped back, smiling innocently as Mrs Trifle came though the door.

'It's okay to move now,' Mrs Trifle said to Selby, wondering why there were flecks of white in the fur on his face. 'Come along, it's time to go home. You've been such a good dog.'

'Are you kidding?' Selby thought. 'I'm a failure. Poor Mrs Trifle is going to be shocked to her socks when she sees that silly sculpture. Oh, well, at least I tried.'

A month later the sculpture came back from the foundry in a big wooden box. People crowded around as Mrs Trifle prised it open.

'This is terrible,' Selby thought. 'They're going to be really upset at Mrs Trifle for spending so much money on a terrible sculpture. I can't watch.'

Selby put a paw over his eyes and then thought of sneaking away when suddenly a big cheer went up.

'Well, they seem to like it,' Selby thought, wondering whether it was okay to look. 'Maybe Sigfried Slapdash was right after all.'

'It's lovely!' cried Mrs Trifle. 'I knew that sculptor could make a good sculpture of a dog if he put his mind to it. And goodness, the face is exactly like Selby's face! Why it's an exact copy.'

Selby slowly pulled his paw away from his face and saw himself looking back.

'It *is* me!' he thought. 'And all because that goo hit me in the face. No wonder it looks just like me. It'll be strange seeing a sculpture of myself right here in the middle of town. It's sort of embarrassing. But I have to admit that when I look at it it makes me feel kind of good.'

THE SKY EYE SPY

'Stars and planets are so exciting!' Selby thought as he listened to the Trifles talk to their old astronomer friend, Percy Peach. 'They're so mysterious. I just love to think of myself out there in the depths of space. It makes me all goosebumpy. Of course I've been to Mars but that's just a nearby planet. It's nothing like going to another galaxy.'

'Whatever happened to that telescope that you had poking up through your garage roof?' Percy asked the Trifles. 'The one we used when we discovered the Peach-Trifle Comet, remember?' ❧

❧ Paw note: See the story 'Selby Soars to New Heights' in the book Selby Speaks. You'll love it! S

'We had to put it away. There were three problems with it,' Dr Trifle explained. 'First of all, that hole in the roof let the rain in. Secondly, I'm not so good at looking through telescopes. I usually only see my own eyelashes — a few stars but mostly dirty great blinking eyelashes.'

'And what was the third problem?' Percy asked.

'We could never find the stars and planets we wanted to find,' Mrs Trifle chimed in. 'We'd look up and see lots of little white dots but we could never tell which one was which. If you ask me, they all ought to have their names next to them so when you look through a telescope you could just read the names.'

'Well it's not possible to put names up in the sky, of course, but I have the next best thing,' Percy said, showing her a copy of his book, *Everyday Stars for You and Me*.

Percy took a map out of a pocket in the back of the book and unfolded it till it covered the dining-room table.

'This is *Percy Peach's Planet Plan*,' he added. 'It's got all the best-known stars and planets with their names printed right next to them.'

'That's very clever,' Mrs Trifle said.

'I'm glad you like it,' Percy said proudly.

'Amateur astronomers tell me that it's a real life-saver. They'd be lost without it.'

'A life-saver, eh? What's on the other side of the map?' Dr Trifle asked. 'There seems to be a whole lot of other stars.'

'One side has the stars that we see from the southern part of the world. The other side has the stars they see in the north.'

'Suddenly I want to get that telescope out again,' Dr Trifle said.

'Hey, I've got an idea!' Percy cried. 'How would you like to look through a proper huge telescope?'

'That sounds like fun,' said Mrs Trifle. 'Which one?'

'Do you know that new telescope, the one they call Sky Eye?'

'The one they sent up in a rocket?' Mrs Trifle asked.

'That's it. Let's have a squiz through it.'

'But how can we do that?' Dr Trifle asked. 'It's way up in space.'

'Yes, but it's controlled from a tracking station on the ground — about a hundred kilometres from here. I know the people there. I'm sure they'll let us use it. There's no one actually up there with the telescope, of course.'

'I don't understand how it works,' Mrs Trifle said.

'Simple: they send up signals to move the telescope this way and that and tell it where and when to take pictures.'

'But how do they see the pictures?' Dr Trifle asked.

'They're sent back through the air — it's all beeps and squeaks and dots and dashes. These go into a computer and the computer de-wonkifies them.'

'It de-whats them?'

'They're usually wonky — all blurry and everything — so they have to be kind of smoothed out before you can actually see them properly. Come on, let's drive out there. We'll take some photos, put them on a disk and then bring the disk back here to look at on your computer.'

'Isn't it amazing what they can do these days? When I was a girl there was none of this fancy stuff,' Mrs Trifle said, and the three of them headed for the car.

'I wish I could go with them,' Selby thought. 'I've read all about the Sky Eye. It would be so much fun discovering new comets and galaxies. Oh well, at least I'll get to see the pictures on the computer later on. Hmmm, I wonder what Percy's book is like.'

Selby lay down on the lounge next to the swimming pool in the backyard and read a chapter on spying in *Everyday Stars for You and Me*.

'Crumbs,' he thought. 'I never knew you could use sky telescopes to spy on people all the way down on the ground. That would be even more fun than looking at the stars! Oh, I love all that spy stuff.' 🐾

As the sun set and as the first stars began to appear, Selby held up *Percy Peach's Planet Plan* to see if he could tell which star or planet was which.

'The problem with this thing,' Selby said, lying on his back and using all four legs to hold the map up, 'is that when I hold the map, I can't see the stars anymore because the map's in the way. I give up. It may be a life-saver for some people but it's only a life-complicator for me.

🐾 *Paw note: I do love spy stuff. For more of my adventures read 'Selby Supersnoop, Dog Detective' in the book* Selby Supersnoop.

Maybe it's better to just look at the stars and planets and not worry about what silly names we've given them.'

Late that night the Trifles and Percy Peach returned.

'I won't stay,' Percy said at the door. 'You can look at the photos by yourselves.'

'But don't you want to see them?' Dr Trifle said.

'I've seen a lot of stars and planets. Besides, I've got to be back in the city by morning and it's a long drive.'

Selby watched as the Trifles excitedly put a diskette into the computer and started looking at all the photos they'd taken with the Sky Eye. There were dry and craggy planets and strange swirling galaxies with lots of colours like exploding fireworks.

'These pictures are so wonderful,' Selby thought. 'They take my breath away.'

'It's all very nice,' Mrs Trifle said finally. 'But I think I like the Earth better than the stars. It's all kind of cold out there and it's nice and warm and cozy down here. I've got an idea: let's have a look at the pictures we took of Bogusville.'

'They took pictures of Bogusville?' Selby

thought. 'They actually turned the telescope around and pointed it down here! Wow! This is going to be fun!'

Dr Trifle found the photo of Australia and then zoomed down to Bogusville. As he zoomed closer and closer Selby could see houses and then people appear.

'The people all look like ants,' Mrs Trifle said. 'Make it bigger so we can see them properly.'

Dr Trifle clicked the computer mouse and made things bigger and bigger.

'Look! There's Aunt Jetty!' Mrs Trifle cried. 'You can see her perfectly. And look! She was picking her nose when we took the photo. She didn't know she was being spied on from space. Isn't that a riot!'

'Yeah, a disgusting riot,' Selby thought. 'That woman gives me the shivers even when she *doesn't* have her finger halfway up her nose. Yuck!'

'Let's zoom in on our house,' Dr Trifle said, moving across the town till the top of the house was in view.

'What's the point?' asked Mrs Trifle. 'There was nobody at home. We were at the tracking station, remember?'

'Maybe we'll see Selby,' Dr Trifle said. 'Maybe he was outside somewhere.'

'Gulp,' Selby thought. 'They were actually spying on me! I'm not sure I like this.'

'Hmmm, I wonder if that's him in the backyard next to the pool?' said Mrs Trifle. 'There's sort of a blob-like thing there on the lounge.'

'Oh, no!' Selby thought as the sweat began to pour down his forehead. 'I was out there reading that stupid book and they were looking down on me! They're going to catch me reading! I'm about to be sprung — from space by that stupid Sky Eye spy!'

'Let's zoom in a little closer,' Mrs Trifle said. 'I can't quite make out what I'm looking at.'

'Oh, woe,' Selby thought. 'This is it. This is the end. The Trifles are about to find out that I'm not just an ordinary non-star-gazing dog but the only real live talking, thinking, book-reading dog in Australia and, perhaps, the world. I might as well tell them before they find out for themselves.'

Selby put his paws up on the computer table and cleared his throat ready to say: 'Okay, okay, turn that silly thing off — you caught me,' when Dr Trifle clicked the computer mouse again.

Suddenly a strange image filled the screen. It was all blue but sprinkled with little white dots.

'Hey, that's not me,' Selby thought. 'It's *Percy Peach's Planet Plan*! — the star map! Just when they took the picture I was holding the star map over my head and that stupid Sky Eye couldn't see me! Thank goodness for that!'

'This is very strange,' Dr Trifle said. 'The telescope must have turned around again. I do believe we're looking back out into space. That's what all those white dots are: they're stars and planets.'

'But there's something very unusual about them,' Mrs Trifle said.

'They just look like stars to me,' Dr Trifle said.

'Except — they have all their names printed next to them. It's just the way it should be,' Mrs Trifle said, looking out the window to see if the names were next to the stars. 'That is the strangest thing I've ever seen.'

'What a close call!' Selby thought as he breathed a sigh of relief and headed off to get a good night's sleep. 'And Percy Peach was dead right: that planet plan of his certainly is a life-saver. Well it saved my life, anyway!'

SELBY'S SALSA

'This Pablito Coco is the greatest bandleader ever!' Selby thought as he whirled around the floor. 'I just love his music! When I hear that beat I've just gotta use my feet. First my tail starts twitching, and my toes start tapping, then my body starts a-boppin' and then I'm up and I'm hoppin' and I'm cruisin' to the music!'

Selby spun across the room as the CD player played a samba, then a rumba, then a mambo, and a tango.

'Dr and Mrs Trifle are so lucky because they can dance with each other. Which is what they're doing right now at their weekly dance class at

> 🐾 Paw note: Salsa music is really boppy dance music — and I just love it!
>
> S

Bogusville Hall. And here am I, the only dancing dog in Australia and, perhaps, the world, with no one to dance with. So,' Selby said, grabbing a mop from the kitchen and turning it stringy-side up, 'how would you like to bop, Molly Mop?'

Selby did a few tango twists and turns before turning out the overhead light and throwing the room into darkness except for the little blinking lights of the CD player.

'It's much better dancing in the dark,' he said, suddenly singing along with the words on the CD. *'Baysa may, baysa may mucho.* I don't know what that means but it sounds sooooo romantic. Oh, oh, I just *love* this next dance! — "The Coco Bongo Longo" — written by the king himself: Pablito Coco. Yes! Yes! Yes!' he hissed, swinging one paw in the air and swivelling his hips to the beat. 'If only the Trifles had an extra long dance class I could dance and dance and dance till I dropped.'

Little did Selby know that the Trifles had had an extra *short* dance class and had just driven into the driveway.

'Listen to that,' Mrs Trifle said as she tangoed down the path to the house. 'We must have left the CD player on. Selby must be going crazy with all that racket in there.'

119

'He seems to like this music,' Dr Trifle said, doing a quick-step up to the front door. 'Today when I was playing it I could have sworn he was smiling and even twitching to the beat.'

'Impossible. Dogs don't smile. And they certainly don't twitch to beats. They only twitch when they're having a bad dream.'

'I know, but that's the way it seemed.'

Unaware that the Trifles were standing in the doorway fumbling for the light switch, Selby whirled the mop around in the dark. Then, just as the blasting bongos of 'The Coco Bongo Longo' reached their peak, Selby did a quick spin and a dip, bending over and puckering up as if to kiss his dancing partner.

'Hey, Molly,' he whispered, 'how about a big juicy smooch for a handsome dancing pooch?'

Suddenly the lights came on and Selby dropped the mop and stood there bent over, frozen with fear.

'Selby!' Mrs Trifle screamed. 'What's going on here? What were you doing?!'

'Oh, no! They've caught me!' Selby screamed in his brain. 'Now they know I'm not an ordinary non-talking non-dancing dog! What am I going to do?!'

'This is terrible!' Mrs Trifle cried, racing to Selby's side. 'He's tripped on that miserable mop and done his back in! Look! He can't move! He's as stiff as a board!'

'That's it!' Selby thought. 'She's given me the perfect excuse! I've done my back in! That's brilliant! I thought I was caught but I'm not!'

'What do you mean he's done his back in?' asked Dr Trifle. 'I think he's put his back *out*.'

'Doing your back in, putting your back out, it means the same thing,' Mrs Trifle explained. 'One of those little doovers in his back has slipped and now he can't move. I think we'd better get him to a vet.'

'But it's nighttime and the vet's closed,' Dr Trifle said. 'Let's just lie him down and let him rest. With any luck his back will be better in the morning and then we won't have to take him to the vet.'

Dr and Mrs Trifle picked Selby up and laid him gently on the lounge.

'He's in so much pain he can't even wag his tail, poor thing,' Mrs Trifle said. 'I've got an idea: let's get Jetty over here.'

'Jetty? What does she know about dogs?'

'She did that course in chiro-whatsis where you learn to crack backs and snap people's spines back into line.'

'But dog backbones aren't like people backbones.'

'Don't be silly — of course they are. The only difference is that dogs' backbones go all the way down to the tips of their tails while ours finish at our bottoms. I'll ring Jetty right now.'

'I hate that woman more than anyone else in the whole world!' Selby thought. 'I just hope she can't come over.'

Selby watched and listened as Mrs Trifle talked to her sister and then put the phone down.

'She'll be here in two minutes,' Mrs Trifle told Dr Trifle. 'I didn't tell her whose back was out of whack because I know she doesn't much care for Selby.'

'And the feeling is mutual,' thought Selby. 'I can't stand the idea of that woman even touching me. What am I going to do?'

Minutes later the dreadful Aunt Jetty bounded into the lounge room cracking her knuckles and then spitting on her hands and rubbing them together.

'Okay,' she said, 'I've got that healin' feelin'. Now who's got the bodgy back?'

'It's not us; it's Selby,' Dr Trifle explained. 'He tripped on a mop and now he can't move at all.'

Aunt Jetty shot Selby an icy stare. 'Not such a

bad thing if you ask me,' she mumbled. 'Why not just leave him that way?'

'Oh, we couldn't do that,' Mrs Trifle said. 'But if you don't think you can help him —'

'What? Of course I can. I'll have him back in shape in a second but I warn you — if that mongrel bites me again,' the woman said, 'I'll have his grotty little guts for garters. Okay, here goes.'

For a minute, Aunt Jetty just ran her fingers gently up and down Selby's spine. Then, before he could even think to blink, she grabbed him around the neck and spun him like a top.

'Merciful heavens!' Selby thought. 'That hurt! That great galumph is so rough! She has hands like hammers! Oh, well, now I can pretend that I'm okay and she'll think she fixed my back.'

But before Selby had a chance to move and stretch and pretend he was okay, Aunt Jetty suddenly said, 'No good. It didn't work.'

'How can you tell?' Mrs Trifle asked.

'I didn't hear it crack. Old Horrible here just flipped over when I wrenched his head around. He's too light. I've got to have a think about this.'

'While you're thinking we'll be changing out

of our dancing gear,' Dr Trifle said. 'These shoes are killing me.'

Once again Aunt Jetty felt her way up and down Selby's spine, tapping it with her knuckles.

'Everything seems to be okay,' she mumbled. 'But obviously it's not or he wouldn't be lying there frozen like an ice cube. Hmmm, Willy and Billy are waiting in the car. Maybe they could help.'

'Oh, no!' Selby screamed in his brain as Aunt Jetty raced out to her car. 'If there's anyone I hate more than Aunt Jetty, it's Billy! And if there's anyone I hate more than Billy, it's Willy!'

'Mummy! Mummy! That's that dog that talks!' Willy cried, as the terrible twosome ran into the room. 'Honest he does!'

'Yes, I'm sure he does.'

'He does! He does! He knows how to talk and he's a liar because he says he can't talk.'

'Never mind about that,' Aunt Jetty said. 'He's got a bad back and I promised my sister I'd fix it. Now grab his back feet and his tail and just hold them still, okay?'

'Oh, goody goody!' Billy squealed. 'His back is broke! His back is broke!'

'Can I twist his tail? Can I?' Willy said, grabbing Selby's tail.

'Just hold tight,' Aunt Jetty said, putting Selby's head in a vice-like headlock.

'Help!' Selby thought. 'What are they doing to me?!'

But before Selby could even cry: 'Please help me, Dr and Mrs Trifle!' Aunt Jetty wrenched his head sideways, twisting his whole body around like she was wringing out a wet towel. Suddenly a sharp pain shot up from the tip of Selby's tail to the top of his neck. Then there was a loud *pop*! Followed by a whole lot of other *pops*!

'Okay, you old flea-bag,' Aunt Jetty said. 'I think that did the trick.'

'Oh great,' Selby thought. 'It did the trick all right: now my spine is completely out of line! Now I really can't move!'

'He's okay now,' Aunt Jetty said, dusting her hands together as Dr and Mrs Trifle came into the room again.

'But — but he's still not moving,' Mrs Trifle said. 'And there's sweat pouring off his forehead. I think he's really in pain now. You didn't fix him, you made him worse.'

'Oh well, you win some and you lose some.

Maybe it's time to get a new dog,' Aunt Jetty said. 'Come along, boys.'

'Get a new dog? But we love Selby,' Mrs Trifle protested.

'I think we broke his back, Mummy,' Billy snorted.

'Serves him right for lying,' Willy giggled. 'Hey, that was really fun!'

Selby lay there in agony watching as Aunt Jetty and her sons disappeared out the door.

'This is awful!' he thought. 'That miserable marrow-mangling monster has ruined my back forever! Why didn't I just tell the Trifles that I'm the only talking and dancing dog in Australia and, perhaps, the world, and get it over with? Of course they'd have put me to work but at least I wouldn't be in this fix. Oh woe woe woe, it's just not fair.'

'I'll take Selby to the vet in the morning,' Mrs Trifle said to Dr Trifle. 'Poor dear. He must be in terrible pain.'

'I'll leave the music on in case he can't sleep,' Dr Trifle said. 'They say that music is the best medicine.'

'If Aunt Jetty ever comes near me again,' Selby thought as he lay on the lounge after the

Trifles had gone to bed, 'I'll bite her into next week! Speaking of biting: there's a flea biting me and I can't even scratch myself! Oh, woe, this is going to be a long night.'

Selby lay there listening as the CD player played a samba, and then a rumba, and then a mambo, and a tango.

'The music does help to take my mind off the pain,' he thought. 'But it also makes me want to dance.'

Slowly the beat built up and up and when the music finally broke into 'The Coco Bongo Longo' the very end of Selby's tail began to twitch. It twitched and it twitched and Selby heard a *pop!* Then a little more of his tail twitched and there was another *pop!* Followed by another and another.

'My back legs!' Selby thought. 'I can move them now! Look at that, they're moving to the music!'

The more he moved, the more his spine popped and then the more he *could* move.

'My spine! My spine!' he squealed. 'It's popping into line! I can feel my tootsies twitching as my feet begin to beat and that *pop-pop-pop*pin's just a-rockin' up my spine! I'm fine! I'm fine!'

Little by little Selby's back loosened and finally he jumped to his feet. In a minute he was dancing around the room as fast as ever.

'This is wonderful!' he thought. 'Dr Trifle was absolutely right: music really is the best medicine!'

SELBY SLUGS AUNT JETTY

Selby had put his mouth down into his bowl and started munching a dog biscuit when suddenly he felt something soft and gooey in his mouth.

'Soft?' Selby thought. 'Gooey? Dry-Mouth Dog Biscuits aren't soft and gooey; they're hard and dry. Oh, no, it's that slug again!' he cried, spitting a mouthful of biscuit and the slug on the floor. 'I had a slug in my mouth! Oh, yuck yuck yuck! Anyway, I'd better get rid of it before Mrs Trifle sees it because she's terrified of slugs. She goes into shock when she sees one.'

Selby picked up the slug, which was still very much alive, and tried to throw it out the window but it stuck to his paw. After three goes, it finally came loose and flew through the air, landing in the bushes at the back of the yard.

'That's the fourth time this week that slug has

got into my bowl. Every time I throw it out the window it comes back. They're such disgusting creatures,' Selby thought as he rinsed some of the slug-slime out of his mouth. 'And there's something weird about them: they move slowly when you're watching them and yet they get around so fast. I reckon they sprout legs and run when no one's looking.'

Selby curled up for an afternoon nap, with the taste of slug still in his mouth.

'I don't mind snails,' he thought, 'but I *hate* slugs. They're so creepy. Hmmm, I feel a snail and slug poem coming on:

> *'Oh little snail*
> *So swift, so frail*
> *How I love your silvery trail*
> *But a slug? — Ugh!'*

Selby dozed off, still chuckling at his poem. In his sleep he dreamt that the slug had shot straight back into the house and climbed up his tail. A short time later Selby awoke with a shudder.

'This is awful!' he thought. 'I've got slugs on the brain. I can't even sleep without dreaming about them!'

'Selby, it's time to go. Come on, get up.'

Selby blinked and then blinked again. Standing

over him was Mrs Trifle, wearing an old-fashioned dress, gloves and a wide-brimmed straw hat. Next to her was Dr Trifle in a dark suit with tails, a tall hat and a huge false moustache. For a moment he thought he'd gone back in time.

'Oh, I forgot: it's the Bogusville Historical Society Dinner tonight,' Selby thought. 'I heard the Trifles say that they were going to take me along with them. Oh, woe, I don't want to go. It's going to be dead boring.'

'Why in the world are you taking old smelly paws to a formal dinner?'

Standing behind the Trifles was Mrs Trifle's dreadful sister, Aunt Jetty, also dressed in old-fashioned clothes.

'Oh no, she's coming too!' Selby thought. 'Why can't they just leave me at home?'

'Do you mean Selby?' Mrs Trifle asked her sister.

'The dog is a living, breathing flea-farm,' Aunt Jetty said. 'And he smells like a sewer. He's full of dog germs. Nobody wants to have dinner with a dog. They'll be throwing up all over the place.'

'Don't be cruel,' Mrs Trifle said. 'The members of the Historical Society specifically asked us to bring him along. They all want to see

Selby next to the statue of Bogus. He was the model for the statue, you know, and the statue is going to be put in the park tomorrow.'

'If you let him near that statue,' Aunt Jetty said, 'he'll probably do his business on it.'

'Jetty! Don't be silly,' Mrs Trifle said. 'Now stop complaining and let's get going.'

'Do my business,' Selby thought. 'I'll do my business on her in a minute. Why does she always have to be so nasty to me? Boy, how I'd like to tell her just what I think of her. Of course that would mean giving away my secret so I'll never be able to do it. Oh, well.'

Bogusville Hall was filled with long tables and lots of people in their finest old-fashioned clothes. On the stage was the statue of Bogus. Mrs Trifle sat Selby next to it while people took photographs but, when the meal started, he lay under the head table munching the dog biscuits that Mrs Trifle had brought for him.

'This is not only boring — it's torture,' Selby thought. 'Here I am eating Dry-Mouth Dog Biscuits while everyone else gets to eat scrummy *people*-food!'

Suddenly Selby sensed something squiggling

133

around on his spine. He turned his head to see but he couldn't turn far enough to see what it was.

'It feels like a bug or something,' he thought, trying not to panic. 'I hope it's nothing bitey — like a big spider. I need a mirror so I can see what it is. I know, I'll just nip into the ladies' loo. There are always lots of mirrors in ladies' loos.'

Selby slipped down the hall and found the door marked 'Ladies'.

'Good,' he thought, opening the door a crack before slipping into the loo. 'I've got the place all to myself. If anyone comes in I can just hide in a toilet thingy till they go out again.'

Selby hopped up on a basin and turned around, looking over his shoulder. Sure enough, there was something on his back. He could see a long slippery trail starting at the tip of his tail and ending at the slug in the middle of his back.

'Crumbs. It's that sticky little slug again!' he thought. 'The flippin' thing *did* climb up my tail while I was sleeping!'

Selby worked his paw up behind him and flicked the slug, sending it high into the air and across the room.

'Good, it's gone,' he thought. 'But I'd better

wipe the slime off my back before someone pats me and gets their hand all gooey.'

Selby dashed into a toilet cubicle, hopped up on a toilet, closed the door, and grabbed a pawful of toilet paper.

'Yucky yuck and double yuck!' he mumbled as he wiped his tail and back with the paper. 'Icky sticky gooey goo!'

Suddenly there was a voice from the next cubicle.

'Are you okay in there?' the woman asked.

Selby stopped wiping and stood stock still, holding his breath.

'Crikey! Whoever she is, she heard me talk!' he thought. 'And she must be wondering what all that yucky yucking and icky sticky gooing is all about.'

'I *said*, are you all right?' the woman demanded.

'Yes,' Selby said, putting on his best woman's voice. 'It's just that I was covered in —' Selby stopped in mid-sentence, thought again and then said: 'I mean I'm perfectly all right.'

'Then could you give me some toilet paper? This one's out.'

Selby started unrolling some toilet paper to let

it fall down where the woman could grab it under the barrier.

'Hey, what do you think of the mayor bringing her *dog* to a formal dinner?' the woman said while she waited.

'Crikey! It's Aunt Jetty!' Selby thought, winding the toilet paper up on the roll again. 'And she's right in the next toot! I should have recognised her voice!'

'Don't you think it's a bit off?' Aunt Jetty added.

'But he had to be here,' Selby said in a high voice. 'He was the model for that lovely statue.'

'Don't remind me,' Aunt Jetty said. 'Now every time I drive by Bogusville Park I'll have to look at the old flea-bag.'

Selby could feel his blood pressure rising.

'Flea-bag? What do you mean by that?' Selby asked. 'He's no flea-bag!'

'Okay, settle down,' Aunt Jetty said. 'You're obviously a mutt-lover. Hey, where's that toilet paper? I thought you were going to give me some.'

'Get it yourself, you great gangling galumph,' Selby said, suddenly forgetting to put on his best woman's voice and sounding like himself again.

'You are the most pig-headed, nasty and stupid person who has ever walked the streets of this town. So there!'

'Hang on, who are you? You're a man, aren't you?! How dare you come into the ladies' loo and insult perfectly innocent, decent ladies — like me. I could have you arrested! What's your name?!'

'My name? I'll tell you my name,' Selby said as he started to leave. 'I'm Selby, the only talking dog in Australia and, perhaps, the world, you — you — you slug-brain!'

'Hey! Come back here! I'm going to find out who you are!'

'You just did,' Selby said with a laugh. 'See ya.'

Selby shot out of the loo, dashed under the table and curled up again feeling delighted with himself.

'That was great,' he thought. 'I finally got to tell her what I thought of her. That was so much fun. I think I'm having a good time after all.'

Soon Selby saw Aunt Jetty's legs re-appear, next to Mrs Trifle's.

'Good gracious,' Mrs Trifle said to her sister. 'You look like you've just seen a ghost.'

'Worse,' Aunt Jetty said. 'I've just seen a man — in the ladies' loo.'

'Really?'

'Yes, and he was very rude to me. He wouldn't give me any toilet paper.'

'You asked a man for toilet paper in the ladies' loo? Are you joking? Who was he? What did he look like?'

'I don't know. I didn't actually see him. He was in the next toot.'

'He was? How can you be sure he was a man if he was in "the next toot", as you say?'

'I know what a man sounds like and he definitely sounded like one. I asked him who he was and he said his name was Selby and that he was a talking dog. Very funny: ha ha.'

'You didn't just imagine this, did you?' Mrs Trifle asked.

'Absolutely not. Cross my heart.'

'I think you were probably just mistaken,' Mrs Trifle said. 'Some women have quite deep voices, you know.'

'You don't believe me, do you?'

'Just eat your ice cream before it melts. We can talk about it later.'

Selby was rolling around under the table, killing himself trying not to laugh. Then, suddenly, he saw the slug — making its way up the outside of Aunt Jetty's dress.

'Hello,' Selby thought, 'there's that slug again. When I flicked it off me, it must have landed on Aunt Jetty. Oh, goody goody — this is going to be great! Just wait till she sees it! She'll scream the roof off!'

Selby rubbed his paws together and watched with delight as the slug made its way up above the tabletop. He put his paws over his ears, waiting for the scream that he knew would come the very moment Aunt Jetty saw — or felt — the creature.

Minutes passed and then more minutes.

'I can't stand it!' he thought, panting to catch his breath. 'It's like waiting for a bomb to go off! But nothing's happening. Come on, come on. Hurry up, sluggy wuggy, do your stuff.'

Selby uncovered his ears.

'This is driving me around the twist! I can't stand it. I've got to see what's happening.'

Selby crept out from under the table and looked at Aunt Jetty who was sitting down busily talking to Mrs Trifle.

'I can't see the slug on her anywhere,' Selby thought. 'Where's it gone?'

Suddenly Selby spied the slug: in the middle of the flower that was pinned to Mrs Trifle's lapel.

'Crikey!' Selby thought. 'It's crawled off Aunt

Jetty and now it's on Mrs Trifle. Poor Mrs T will go into shock when she sees it! I've got to get it off her! But how?'

Selby's brain went into top gear.

'I know, I'll bump the table underneath so hard that people's bowls of ice cream will fall over and spill. Then — while Mrs Trifle is distracted — I'll grab her flower. If I'm quick about it, she won't notice a thing.'

Then Dr Trifle looked at Mrs Trifle's flower.

'He's obviously seen the slug,' Selby thought, 'and he'll quietly pick it off the flower so she doesn't notice.'

'What a pretty flower,' Dr Trifle said, putting his face down close to it. 'I wonder if it smells as good as it looks.'

Dr Trifle leaned over and sniffed Mrs Trifle's flower.

'Mmmm, that's lovely,' he said, drawing back.

'Bad luck,' Selby thought. 'He didn't notice the slug. But, hang on — where is it? It's not on her flower anymore. It's disappeared again!'

But not for long. In a moment Selby saw the slug, clinging to Dr Trifle's moustache.

'Oh, no!' Selby screamed in his brain. 'It's dangling down right under his nose. It looks like a

greebie that came out of his nose! Everyone's going to see it in a second! How embarrassing!'

Selby's mind went into top gear once again. In a flash he'd grabbed the pepper shaker and ducked down under the table again.

'This should do it,' Selby thought as he filled his paw with pepper and then blew it up to where Dr Trifle was sitting. 'That slug won't be hanging onto his moustache for long.'

141

Selby saw the doctor's body shake and quake and shudder. Then there were some 'Ah ah ah ah's' followed by a huge 'Chooooooooooooooooo!' which nearly sent Dr Trifle sailing out of his chair.

Selby looked up to see Dr Trifle sticking his slugless moustache back on his upper lip.

'It worked! My plan worked! He sneezed it off. It's gone forever. Now I can relax,' Selby sighed. 'This has been kind of fun after all. It certainly hasn't been boring. I got to tell Aunt Jetty off and I got rid of that pesky little slug. But now I'm exhausted. I can't wait to get home and have a good night's sleep.'

On the way home, Selby was dozing off as he listened to Mrs Trifle and Aunt Jetty.

'What did you think of the food?' Mrs Trifle asked.

'Are you kidding?' Aunt Jetty replied. 'The food's always terrible at these dinners. The best part was the topping on the ice cream.'

'Topping? What topping? I just had a plain old scoop of ice cream with nothing on it.'

'You didn't have a thingy on top?'

'No. What kind of thingy?'

'A marshmallowy sort of thingy,' Aunt Jetty said. 'It was the tastiest part of the whole meal.'

'Oh, no!' Selby thought. 'I think she's talking about the slug.'

'What exactly did this marshmallowy thingy taste like?' Mrs Trifle asked.

'Well it wasn't sweet,' said Aunt Jetty. 'And it was sort of soft and gooey. It really was out of this world. I could have a whole plate full of them.'

'I can't believe it! Aunt Jetty *ate* the slug!' Selby thought, trying not to laugh out loud. 'Oh, this is the perfect ending to a perfect day! I'm so glad the Trifles took me to the dinner. I haven't had so much fun in years!'

SELBY SNOWBOUND
SELBY'S ULTIMATE ADVENTURE

'What do you think is the tallest mountain in the world?' asked the Trifles' mountaineer friend, Wilfred Crampon, as he paced back and forth in his huge mountaineering boots.

'Is this a trick question?' Mrs Trifle asked.

'Absolutely not.'

'Mount Everest, of course. Everyone knows that.'

'Wrong, wrong and double wrong,' the mountaineer said. 'Everyone *thinks* that Mount Everest is the tallest mountain in the world but it most definitely is not.'

'Surely it's been measured, Crampy,' Dr Trifle said, using Wilfred Crampon's nickname.

'Of course it's been measured. But you can't tell if a mountain is the tallest by just measuring *it*.'

'Why not?'

'Simple dimple: you not only have to measure *it* but also every other mountain in the world to see if there's a higher one,' the mountaineer explained.

'Crampy's got a point,' Selby thought as he lay on the carpet listening to the conversation and trying to keep his tail out of the way of Crampy's boots.

'So you're saying that there's a mountain that's never been measured but that you think is taller than Mount Everest?' said Mrs Trifle.

'I *know* it is!'

'But how could the mountain measurers have missed it?' Dr Trifle asked.

'Simp dimp: they never noticed it. You see it's in the farthest corner of Antarctica. I discovered it three months ago when I was on my One-Man-Across-Antarctica expedition. I was zipping along on my snow-mobile when suddenly *bang*! There it was smack dab in front of me! For a minute I thought I had a touch of mountain madness.'

'Mountain madness?' Dr Trifle asked.

'People who spend a lot of time in freezing cold snowy places sometimes see things that aren't there. But the mountain definitely was there and I've got pictures to prove it.'

'So then you whipped out one of those measuring telescope things,' Dr Trifle said excitedly, 'and measured it and then made trigonometric calculations and — Bob's your uncle — you found out that it was taller than Mount Everest! Great work, Crampy!'

'Well . . . not exactly,' Crampy Crampon said, scratching his scraggly beard.

'I beg your pardon?'

'Bob wasn't my uncle. I mean I didn't have one of those measuring thingies. And, besides, I'm hopeless at trigono-whatsis.'

'But you're sure it's higher than Mount Everest?'

'I can tell by just looking at it. It's really really really really really *really* tall!' Crampy said, raising his hand up and almost hitting the ceiling. 'Which is at least one *really* taller than Mount Everest.'

'I've got an idea,' said Mrs Trifle. 'Just tell everyone about the mountain. Someone is bound to dash down to Antarctica to measure it properly.'

'Not on your life! They might climb it too. And I want to be the first to climb it.'

'You want to climb it?' Dr Trifle said.

'Well, I *am* a mountaineer and it *is* a mountain.

Hey, I've got an idea!' Crampy cried. 'Let's all go to Antarctica!'

'Are you serious?' Dr and Mrs Trifle said at exactly the same time.

'Deadly,' said Crampy. 'You can make those trigono-whatsis calculations while I climb the mountain. It'll be the ultimate adventure.'

'The ultimate adventure?' Mrs Trifle said. 'Doesn't *ultimate* mean *last*?'

'It also means the best. This is going to be the greatest adventure ever!'

'That sounds great but when would we go?'

'How about Wednesday?'

'So soon?'

'My TV program about crossing Antarctica is about to be on TV and when people see Mount Crampon there'll be mountaineers from all over the world racing down there to be the first to climb it.'

'Mount Crampon?' Mrs Trifle said. 'You've named it after yourself.'

'Well, not yet. To get a mountain named after you you have to be the first person to climb it and then you leave your name at the top. It's an old tradition.'

With this Crampy Crampon whipped a flag out of his pocket that said:

'Oh, and bring Selby along,' Crampy added. 'Dogs are good luck on expeditions. I'm sure he'll like it.'

'Like it? I'll love it!' Selby screamed in his brain. 'Oh boy, oh boy, oh boy! I get to go on a real live Antarctic expedition! Look out icebergs! Look out penguins! Look out mountains! Here I come!'

So it was that on the following Wednesday, Crampy Crampon, Dr and Mrs Trifle, and Selby found themselves winging their way towards Antarctica in Crampy's own personal ski-plane with the mountaineer at the controls.

'The race is on,' Crampy said. 'Everybody saw my TV show last night and now hundreds of mountaineers are planning to go to Antarctica and climb Mount Crampon. Fortunately, they don't know exactly where it is so we'll have a good head start.'

Selby sat covered from head to paw in the special mountaineers' cold weather clothes that Mrs Trifle had made for him.

'This is sooooo exciting!' Selby thought. 'Look at all that snow down there! I can't wait to make a snowdog!'

The plane flew deep into Antarctica and slid to a stop high up on a glacier just below the peak of the mammoth mountain.

'Okay,' Crampy said as he started off, 'you stay with the plane. You can measure the mountain while I climb it.'

'Okay, Crampy,' Dr Trifle said.

'And if it gets windy while I'm gone don't forget to tie the plane down. Oh and look out for crevasses.'

'Crevasses?' Dr Trifle said.

'Yes, those big deep cracks in a glacier. First rule of mountaineering: don't fall in one. Okay, guys, I'll see ya when I see ya.'

Crampy Crampon climbed up and up and for the first hour, Dr Trifle pointed a measuring telescope at the top of the mountain and then down to the valley below. Then he made lots of trigono-something calculations.

'I'm afraid Crampy is going to be bitterly disappointed,' Dr Trifle said finally as he blew on his hands to warm them up. 'The mountain isn't as high as Mount Everest. It's just a tad shorter.'

'Exactly how much of a tad shorter is it?' Mrs Trifle asked.

'Well not even a tad — a tiny fraction of a tad. If my calculations are correct Mount Everest is just forty-three centimetres taller than Mount Crampon.'

'That's too bad,' Selby thought. 'Oh, well, at least Crampy will be the first to climb the *second* highest mountain in the world.'

All day long the Trifles watched the mountaineer through binoculars as he climbed up and up the steep slope. But then, just as Crampy was nearing the top, a wind came up. Within minutes the whole mountain had disappeared in clouds of blowing snow.

'I think we'd better tie the plane down before the wind hits us too,' Mrs Trifle said, grabbing some spikes and ropes.

Selby watched from inside the tiny plane as the Trifles struggled against the freezing wind, tying more and more ropes to the plane to keep it from blowing away.

'There are times when it's good to be a dog,' he thought. 'And one of those times is when there's freezing cold work to do.'

Suddenly there was a crackle on the radio.

'Help! Can anyone hear me?' Crampy's voice cried. There was a long pause and then: 'I didn't make it to the top and now the wind just blew my goggles away and my eyes are icing up! I can't see a thing! This could be the last time you hear from me! Goodbye, good Trifles! Goodbye!'

'Oh, no! What am I going to do?!' Selby said aloud. 'I've got to tell the Trifles! But what can *they* do?! They're not mountaineers any more than I am. And without Crampy we're doomed! We need him to fly the plane.'

Selby looked out just in time to see a gust of wind blow Dr and Mrs Trifle end over end across the glacier. In a second *they'd* disappeared.

'This is a disaster!' Selby cried. 'I need to save Dr and Mrs Trifle but I can't go out there or I'll be blown away too.'

Minutes passed and then Selby suddenly spied Crampy Crampon's copy of *The Mountaineer's Rescue Manual*. His eyes scanned the pages desperately looking for something — anything — that might help.

'This is stupid,' he thought, finally. 'I can't just sit here reading a book. I've got to get out there and see if I can find the Trifles. I only wish I was more of a rescuing type of dog instead of a sitting around and watching TV one. Oh well, here goes.'

Selby put on his thick gloves and goggles and pulled his hood down tight around his face. He grabbed a rope and tied it to the seat of the plane and climbed out. The blast of wind almost blew him away but he clung tight to the rope and, little by little, let it out until he was well behind the plane. Soon he came to a shallow crevasse and, looking down, he saw the Trifles lying motionless at the bottom.

Selby threw a special mountaineer's ladder into the crevasse and climbed down.

'The Trifles are alive!' he thought as he could see they were still breathing. 'But the fall must have knocked them out. I can't possibly lift them so I'll have to wake them up and get them to climb out.'

Selby shook them and watched as they slowly opened their eyes.

'Where am I?' Mrs Trifle said suddenly.

'I don't know,' Dr Trifle said. 'We seem to be lying on the ground somewhere. There's ice and snow all around. I don't think we're in Bogusville.'

Selby cleared his throat and said: 'Okay, guys. You've got to get out of here before you freeze to death, okay?'

'I beg your pardon?' Mrs Trifle said. 'Selby, did you just speak?'

'Yes, I did. Now just see if you can get to your feet and —'

'When did you learn to talk?' Dr Trifle interrupted.

'A long time ago,' Selby said. 'Now come on —'

'Exactly how *did* you learn to talk?'

'I was just watching TV with you and suddenly I could understand everything that was being said,' Selby said. 'But never mind about that —'

'Then you've been listening to our conversations for years,' Mrs Trifle said, struggling to her feet. 'You've heard all of our most private conversations — all those embarrassing things.'

'I tried not to listen,' Selby said.

153

'But why didn't you tell us sooner?' Dr Trifle said.

Selby felt himself getting impatient.

'Never mind! Now get to your feet, you two, and climb out of here and get back in the plane! That's an order!'

Slowly the dumbfounded Trifles climbed up the ladder and struggled back to the plane just as the wind died down again.

'Okay, now, you stay right here while I see if I can rescue Crampy,' Selby said. 'He's lost his goggles and he's freezing to death.'

'B-B-But he's way up on the mountain,' Dr Trifle protested.

'And you're only a dog,' Mrs Trifle reminded him.

'I know that,' said Selby, 'but someone's got to rescue him and you're in no shape to do it. So while the weather is good, I'll just have to give it a go. Wish me luck,' Selby said before closing the door to the plane and heading off.

Selby fought his way up the peak. Finally he saw a red dot lying in the snow just below the highest point on the mountain. Another hour passed until he reached the half-frozen figure of the mountaineer.

'Okay,' Selby said, brushing the snow off the mountaineer's face. 'Let's make this easy on both of us. I'm Selby. I'm also a talking dog — and never mind how I learned to talk or any of that guff. You're a mountain-climber who needs help. So I'm here to rescue you. Got it?'

Crampy opened his eyes and stared up at Selby. A sudden smile spread across his face.

'Mountain madness,' he muttered.

'I beg your pardon?'

'I've got mountain madness. This is what happens to mountaineers when they get stuck out in the cold for too long. They start seeing talking dogs.'

'Have it your way,' Selby said. 'Can you walk?'

Crampy struggled to his feet and then fell on his face.

'Well I guess that answers that,' Selby said. 'Okay, now I'm going to put a rope around you and pull you back down, okay?'

'But I didn't get to the top yet,' Crampy protested. 'It's just up there — a couple of metres more.'

'Forget it,' Selby said. 'We're getting out of here. Anyway, Dr Trifle says it's shorter than Mount Everest.'

'Oh bum,' said the disappointed climber.

155

Selby got out a length of rope, tied it around Crampy, and began pulling the man. But just then, the full force of the storm hit.

'Careful!' Crampy yelled. 'Don't go down right there — there's a cliff. Better go up over that hump up ahead and then go down.'

'Right you are,' Selby said pulling Crampy uphill, helped by a blast of wind.

'I've got to stop,' the exhausted Selby said finally. 'I once saw a TV show about Eskimos making igloos. Let's see if I can remember what they did.'

Selby got a knife out of Crampy's backpack and quickly cut some slabs of hard snow. He made them into an igloo around Crampy. Then he climbed in and sealed up the doorway.

'You're very clever — for a dog,' Crampy said. 'I don't think I've met a dog quite like you.'

'No, you wouldn't have,' Selby said, still panting.

'It's a pity that you're only in my imagination. The real Selby is back at the plane with the Trifles. He can't talk, of course.'

'Of course not,' Selby agreed.

'But don't be offended,' Crampy said. 'You're still good company.'

'Thanks, so are you.'

'You do know that if this storm keeps up we'll freeze to death?'

'I know,' Selby sighed. 'Then it really will be our ultimate adventure.'

Crampy thought for a moment and then burst into laughter.

'And you've got a great sense of humour, too. I like that in a dog.'

The hours rolled by until the sun set but the storm raged on. Selby got colder and colder until he could hardly think. Then, sometime in the early morning he had a terrible thought.

'What if we freeze to death (*sniff*) and they come looking for our frozen bodies and they can't even find us under the snow?' he thought. 'I've got to put a marker out.'

The only thing Selby could find to write on was Crampy's flag. So underneath the words 'Mount Crampon', Selby scribbled:

He struggled out of the igloo and planted the flag in the snow. He then went back inside, sealed up the doorway again, and waited for the cold to put an end to his short life.

But no sooner had he done this than there was a sudden break in the weather. Selby pushed his way outside again and looked around.

'Goodness me!' he exclaimed. 'I made the igloo at the worst possible place — we're right on the top of the mountain! And, look! I can see the plane way down there on the glacier. Quick, Crampy! Wake up! We're getting out of here — now!'

Selby dragged the unconscious mountaineer out of the igloo and started pulling him on the snow down the slope. The slope got steeper and steeper and, suddenly, Selby and Crampy were sliding out of control down the mountain.

'Oh, no!' Selby screamed. 'All this work to save ourselves and now we're going to be killed!'

Over and over the two bounced and slid their way down the slope until they came to a stop at the aeroplane.

'I've got to get into the plane and w-w-w-warm up. I'm f-f-f-f-freezing!' Selby thought as he opened the door and crawled into the back

behind the sleeping Trifles. He awoke a short time later to the sound of voices.

'Poor Selby,' Mrs Trifle said. 'He was such a good dog.'

'Yes,' sniffed Dr Trifle. 'And now he's lost forever up there on that stupid mountain. I only wish we'd known he could talk. We could have given him a much better life.'

'Yes, by making him work,' Mrs Trifle said.

'He could have done the cleaning,' Dr Trifle said, 'and the laundry and the ironing and the cooking and washing up. He could have washed the windows and made all the beds every day.'

'Yes, we could have given him a *purpose*. He could have felt really *useful*. He could have been our dogsbody. 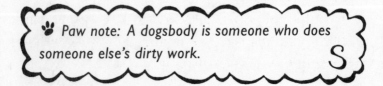 Instead he was probably lying around feeling guilty all the time for not helping out.'

'Guilty, schmilty,' thought Selby. 'I save their lives and now all they can think about is ruining mine!'

Paw note: A dogsbody is someone who does someone else's dirty work. S

Suddenly the plane door opened and Crampy was standing there.

'Crampy!' Mrs Trifle exclaimed. 'Where did you come from?'

'I — I don't know. I think I fell off the mountain. I don't remember much. Would you believe that I actually thought that Selby came up to rescue me and he talked to me?' Crampy laughed.

'It's true!' Dr Trifle exclaimed. 'He talked to us too.'

Crampy let out a long laugh.

'You mean you *think* he did,' Crampy said. 'I'm afraid that you had mountain madness, too.'

'You mean he didn't talk to us?' Mrs Trifle said. 'But it seemed so real.'

'It always does,' said Crampy. 'See, there he is sleeping in the back of the plane.'

'Why so he is. He must have been here all along,' Dr Trifle said.

'By the way, did you measure the mountain?'

'Yes, I'm sorry but it's slightly shorter than Mount Everest.'

'Would you do me a favour?' Crampy said. 'Could you measure it again. You might have just *thought* you measured it.'

Dr Trifle made some more measurements and then did his calculations again.

'Well I'll be,' he said. 'It really *is* higher than Everest. And I can just barely make out your flag up there. That's funny, I didn't notice that roundy bit on top of the peak before. I thought it was more pointy than roundy.'

'I guess my igloo is now part of the mountain,' Selby thought, 'which is just tall enough to make the mountain the highest one in the world.'

'Okay, let's get out of here before another storm hits,' Crampy said, jumping into the plane and starting the engine. 'I don't know about you but even Bogusville seems a nice place to me right now.'

'Not just a nice place,' Selby thought. 'But the nicest place in the whole world.'

But that's not the end of the story. When Selby and Crampy and the Trifles got back, their story was flashed around the world on TV, radio and in the newspapers. Of course Selby lived in fear that someone would climb the mountain again and find his note on Crampy's flag and then the world would know that Selby's talking wasn't mountain madness after all. And soon some climbers did get to the top and the name of the mountain was entered into the *Official Mountain Registry* — but not as Mount Crampon.

The expedition found the flag right where Selby had put it: on top of the igloo, on the top of the mountain. But the wind had ripped it so badly that most of Selby's writing was gone. There were only two strips of cloth left. They said:

'Isn't that a scream?' Mrs Trifle said. 'Crampy must have changed the flag and named it after Selby when he had mountain madness.'

'I can't believe it!' Selby thought. 'Of course I am the one who made it the highest mountain in the world so I guess I deserve having it named after me. But I wish I'd written Mount Trifle on that flag. They're the ones who really deserve it. Oh well, I guess I can live with it.'

This is a silly poem by me.
Read it out loud and get someone
else to say the 'Toy Boat' bits
as fast as they can.

The Toy Boat

I found a little wooden boat
But then I found it wouldn't float.
I said, '**Toy boat toy boat toy boat**
Why won't you float **toy boat toy boat?**'

'Hang on!' I thought, 'You silly goat!
This needs some water first to float!'
Faster **Toy boat toy boat toy boat toy boat
Toy boat toy boat toy boat.**

I jumped into my overcoat
And dived into a castle moat.
I hoped and prayed my boat would float.
'My boat!' I cried. 'Please float please float.'
Even faster **Toy boat toy boat toy boat toy boat
Toy boat toy boat toy boat.**

Which it did. Perfectly. No worries.

So if you want your boat to float
Just quickly quote this rhyme by rote:

Very very fast **Toy boat toy boat toy boat**
Toy boat toy boat toy boat
Toy boat toy boat toy boat toy boat
Toy boat toy boat toy boat!

Hene's an even sillier poem by me.
I hope you like it.

Wrong-headed Luke

A boy named Luke in my home town
Can put his head on upside-down.
His mouth is up, his eyes are down
His happy smile becomes a frown.
And if you think that isn't weird
His spiky hair's a short black beard.

He puts his hat upon his chin
And when it rains his nose drips in.
As you'd expect this makes him wheeze
And cough and snort and even sneeze.
He blows his nose and up it goes
Like water from a garden hose.

And when he's drinking from a cup
Luke lets his drool go running up
Across his lip, just past his nose,
Into his eye this liquid goes
He cries: 'Oh goody look at me!
I can wash my eyes with Luke-warm tea!'

Selby

CLIMATE

In that last story about the
mountain, did you really think
I was going to **climate**?....
especially in such a cold
climb it? I never thought
I could, but I did!

Anyway, now I can sit back
and take it easy again. I just
hope I can get some peace
and quiet before some other
scarey adventure comes
along and threatens to give
away my secret.

So that's all from your
very special dog-friend.

Cya layda,

Selby

ABOUT THE AUTHOR

Duncan Ball began work as an industrial chemist but he'd always wanted to be a writer or a painter. In his spare time he wrote an adult novel and soon he'd given away work in science to began writing the popular books for children that he now writes full time.

Duncan's second novel, a children's book, *Selby's Secret*, exploring the wonderful world of Selby (the only talking dog in Australia and, perhaps, the world), proved such a success that its fans demanded more and more Selby adventures — which Duncan has been happy to supply. The Selby saga now comprises six collections of nearly one hundred short stories (all beautifully illustrated by Allan Stomann), and the musical play, *Selby the Talking Dog*. The Selby books have been published overseas in New Zealand, Japan, Germany and the USA and have won and been short-listed for many awards — most of them voted by the children themselves.

Duncan has also written other books for children including three books about Emily Eyefinger (who was born with an eye on the end of her finger), three books about the diabolical tricks of the cunning and cranky ghost of Arnold Taylor (including *The Ghost and the Goggle Box*), six easy-to-read 'Skinny Mysteries' (including *The Case of the Graveyard Ghost*), and some picture books (including the ever-popular *Jeremy's Tail*, illustrated by Donna Rawlins).

When Duncan isn't writing books for children he is working on television scripts, painting, bushwalking or answering the many letters he receives from children. (To reach him write to him care of HarperCollins at the address in the front of this book.)

For more information about Duncan and his books boot up your computer and surf your way to Selby's website at: http://www.selby.aust.com — see you there!